Mr. Smithson's Bones

Also by Richard Timothy Conroy
The India Exhibition

Mr. Smithson's Bones

A Mystery at the Smithsonian

RICHARD TIMOTHY CONROY

ST. MARTIN'S PRESS   NEW YORK

Library of Congress Cataloging-in-Publication Data

Conroy, Richard Timothy.
    Mr. Smithson's bones / Richard Timothy Conroy.
        p.   cm.
    "A Thomas Dunne book."
    ISBN 0-312-09341-1
    1. Smithsonian Institution—Fiction.   2. Museums—Washington (D.C.)—Employees—Fiction.   I. Title.
    II. Title: Mister Smithson's bones.
PS3553.051985M7   1993
813'.54—dc20   93-4108
                                                       CIP

First Edition: August 1993

10 9 8 7 6 5 4 3 2 1

Foreword

This is a story of murderous doings in the Smithsonian Institution. These deeds have not happened, and may never happen, although one can never be quite certain about that. The staff that takes part in this story does not exist, and may never exist, but one can't be sure about that either.

The Smithsonian is at the center of things in Washington, D.C., situated as it is within walking distance, both literally and figuratively, from the government. It retains, nevertheless, a bit of the tranquil, perhaps academic, feeling—a place where scholars and other professionals go about doing the work they love best, in the institution that makes it possible to do so. The Smithsonian has a benign public face that is almost as well known across the land as the Post Office or this or that national fast-food chain.

It is, in fact, an unlikely place for murder to happen, although it is a lovely place for a murder if you feel you have to have one. Or more. For the Smithsonian is also a world unto itself, as insular as a college, and a place where dark deeds might be imagined to occur, if you care to, and we do.

The author has superimposed upon the Smithsonian a totally fictional cast of characters who are reported as doing completely fictional things. The author, while familiar with the most recent two decades of the Smithsonian, is yet unaware that any murder has ever happened within its confines. Nor is he acquainted with any murderous or other criminal intent on the part of real persons associated with the Smithsonian.

This story is presented as taking place about twenty years ago. The choice of this time is not intended to associate it with the real people who served the Smithsonian with distinction during those years. To the extent that real persons may wish to assume that they played a part in this story, they have the author's assurance that they are mistaken and that they may take no blame nor indeed any credit from this bit of fiction.

Apart from the fiction of this book, the author has endeavored where possible to describe the Smithsonian Institution as it was about 1970. The story, however, has made it necessary here and there to anticipate by some years things such as technical innovations in the field of museum collections management and to shift by a few years certain events that were important in suggesting the plot of this novel.

Further, as fiction, these adventures of Henry Scruggs precede those chronicled in *The India Exhibition—A Mystery at the Smithsonian,* published by St. Martin's Press in August 1992.

Dramatis Personae

(In order of appearance)

All are members of the staff of the Smithsonian Institution unless otherwise specified. All are, of course, fictional.

John Armour Kraft—Assistant Secretary for Science; an ornithologist by profession.

A Murderer

Henry Scruggs—A State Department Foreign Service Officer on loan to the Smithsonian Institution; divorced, lonely, and forty-two.

Olive Blue—Secretary to Dr. Kraft.

Sally Wiggins—Foreign Affairs Specialist, Foreign Affairs Office; deals with passports and visas.

Hamilton Sealyham—Director of Conferences; an anthropologist by profession.

Mr. Taggart—Guard at the East Door of the Castle. By tradition, he wears a black funeral suit rather than a uniform, and regards himself as a major domo rather than a guard.

Dreamy (Dora) Weekes—Director of the Foreign Currency Program; a flirt.

Ambassador (retired) Steuben Craddock—Director, Foreign Affairs Office.

Harlan Whitfield—Secretary of the Smithsonian and an eminent invertebrate biologist (specialty, Gastropoda).

Dr. Hans Christian Fabricius—a Danish postdoctoral fellow in physical anthropology; also a computer hacker.

Dr. O. Arlington Mayes—Emeritus Senior Physical Anthropologist, Museum of Natural History.

Rossmore Owens—Under Secretary at the Smithsonian.

Phoebe Casey—Assistant General Counsel.

Dr. Ulysses Ossum—Chairman of Anthropology, Museum of Natural History.

Col. (U. S. Army, retired) Vince McKeown—Director of the Office of Protection Services.

Bobby Bader—Curator of the Smithsonian Castle; an architectural historian by profession.

William Wright (a.k.a. Bill of Rights)—General Counsel.

Dr. Carleton Parkes—Director of the Natural History Museum.

Dillyhay Plover—Director of Public Affairs.

Gerald Blackman—Foreign Affairs Officer in the Foreign Affairs Office.

Ronald Hipster—Foreign Affairs Officer, deputy director of the Foreign Affairs Office.

Dr. Rebecca Haas—Assistant Director of the Smithsonian Institution Libraries for Exchanges.

Taylor Maidstone—Maker of anthropological films and South Asian specialist.

Percy Jammers—Director of University Programs.

Mr. Carl Harrison—a *Washington Post* reporter, Metro section.

Dillard Haley—Treasurer.

Hayward Bodde (a.k.a. Habeas Corpus)—Associate General Counsel.

Dr. Ezra Fairburn—Director of American Studies at the Smithsonian.

Dr. Carson—Director of Consumer Applications, U.S. Atomic Energy Commission, Germantown, Maryland.

Algernon Teddie—Supervisor, IPES (International Publications Exchange Service).

Douglas (a.k.a. Double) Cross—Assistant Secretary for Museums.

Hannah Norton—Staff Director for the Secretary of the Smithsonian.

Arlington Savage—Chairman, Executive Committee, Board of Regents.

Mr. Smithson's Bones

# One

On a Friday afternoon in early August, Dr. Kraft was working late. It was something he did not like to do, and indeed something he rarely did. He would have been happier about it if he could have kept his secretary after hours to work with him. He did not particularly like Olive and certainly did not lust after her. She wasn't his type. In more ways than one. The fact that he was popularly supposed to be having an affair with Olive showed how little people understood him, especially here at the Smithsonian.

People probably assumed what they did about him and Olive because she was so fiercely protective of him. She would, she made it quite clear, do anything for him. That, of course, was the reason he had brought her with him from the California Institute of Life Sciences when Harlan became Secretary of the Smithsonian and invited him to come with him to head up Science. He supposed that if he should ask Olive to murder someone for him she would do it as readily and efficiently as she did everything else. It was fortunate for his enemies, and it seemed that there were many of them, that he had other and better ways of getting rid of them. Ways that were professionally, if not personally, lethal.

Dr. Kraft rolled a sheet of paper into Olive's typewriter and started to type a letter. He used to be able to type, sort of. Thank God it was nothing he had had to do very often since his days as a graduate student. He pushed down the *shift* key and then struck the *M* key. Nothing happened. For a moment he couldn't figure out why and then he realized that the typewriter was an electric one. He looked around for the *ON* switch. He didn't see any, but there was a little window which showed the power was *OFF*. He felt underneath the typewriter and his fingers encountered the switch. Immediately there was the pulsing sound of a small electrical motor. How could Olive stand the noise when she was trying to think? But of course she didn't actually think, did she?

It was slow but he persevered and made progress. Some keys he found right away, but others like *e, r, i, o,* and *p* had to be hunted down. He decided the trouble was his bifocals. He could never be a typist, not that that was anything requiring an apology. Damn Olive to insist on having a vacation! Of course he had planned to be abroad, and he supposed, to be fair, she couldn't have known he would be back two weeks early.

And damn the Ceylonese for revoking his research permit! How they could take exception to his collecting a few birds was incomprehensible. It still rankled him to think about what the Director General of Forests and Wildlife had said to him when he appealed his permit revocation. *"We here in Ceylon see no purpose to be served by having you people from the Smithsonian Institution shoot our birds to find out why they are becoming extinct."* The nerve of that little jumped-up clerk! He was actually laughing at me! He ought to be glad to have Ceylon* mentioned in the world scientific literature. It surely must be rare enough!

It was probably all the fault of the Smithsonian's Foreign Affairs Office. Those parasitic, failed diplomats should have anticipated the troubles in Ceylon and should have had our embassy in Colombo apply some pressure on the Ceylonese government. And if he had still had his official passport, that

---

*Ceylon is the former name of Sri Lanka.

grinning little flunky in Ceylon would never have treated him the way he did. Not likely. He would blame it on FAO, anyway, particularly that petty martinet Scruggs. One of these days he would talk the Secretary into abolishing FAO, his "little State Department," and there would be a bunch of positions up for grabs. He could use another deputy so he wouldn't have to work late.

Dr. Kraft purged Ceylon and the Foreign Affairs Office from his mind and set himself to destroying a minor Smithsonian official. He was sorry his letter had some mistakes in it. Olive had very high standards. She wouldn't have let this letter pass. Once, he recalled, Olive had refused to accept a letter prepared by another office for his signature. Their typewriter had printed the commas too light. Before they could prepare a new letter, an opportunity was missed and a project went down the tube. Dr. Kraft smiled. Too damn many projects anyway.

Wonder of wonders! He actually found an envelope. He addressed it by hand, and printed PERSONAL—CONFIDENTIAL in large block letters.

He looked once more through his mail. He decided that everything else could wait until he returned to work a week from Monday. No, perhaps he should write a short note to the Secretary while he was sitting on top of his anger about Ceylon. He could be more colorful now than he could be on a busy workday. His anger would burn deep and long later but the clean blue flame would be gone. He had seen it happen before.

He was getting the hang of typing now. He rolled a clean sheet of paper into the machine and began to type: "August 7th   Harlan— We have to face up to the problem of the Foreign Affairs Office. I am just back from Ceylon where—" No, that might seem petty and vengeful. He tore the sheet from the typewriter and crumpled it up. Better to seem to be written before going to Ceylon, predicting what has now come to pass.

He inserted a fresh sheet of paper and began again to type:

July 10th
Harlan—
We have to face up to the problem of the Foreign Affairs
Office. I am just about to go out to South Asia and because
of unnecessary bureaucracy, I have been set up for disas-
ter. We have brought this upon ourselves by harboring
FAO in our midst. It is an office that does not and perhaps
cannot share the Smithsonian's mission . . .

Dr. Kraft typed away, warming to his subject.

He put his note to the Secretary in an envelope and misaddressed it to the Director of the Freer Gallery. Then he tore the envelope open and resealed it with Scotch tape. With a pencil, he redirected the envelope to the office of the Secretary. He buried it under other mail in Olive's OUT box. Anybody would believe it took those idiots over at the Freer a month to send his memo on to the Secretary, and since the Secretary and the Director of the Freer never spoke to each other, the subject would never be mentioned.

Dr. John Armour Kraft, Smithsonian Assistant Secretary for Science, his nasty work done, walked back into his darkened office. He bent over his desk and rested his weight on his desk blotter. He looked out across his empty chair and through the tall, thin, stone-edged windows onto the Mall. It was six weeks after the summer solstice and it was still light, but the color was fading and only the dome of the Museum of Natural History across the way still showed the red tinge of the setting sun. It was a view he particularly liked and it was at its best at this time of year.

Kraft was tired. The flight had taken more than seven hours from London. He was thankful he had gone first class. The accounting people would yell about it but he would shout them down. Lord knows, there were few enough perks to being an Assistant Secretary.

The Smithsonian Castle was quiet now. Friday evenings in the summertime you could walk off with the place and no one would notice. He had gotten to the Castle just as everybody was leaving the building, and had discovered he didn't

4

have his building pass with him. There had been a relief guard on the desk when he came in. Kraft didn't know him, so he entered the offices through the Great Hall, just before the public entrance closed for the day. He knew that nobody ever checked passes that way.

He had intended just to look at his accumulated mail, but there had been this letter that needed immediate action. The others who were involved with this matter might not wait a week for him to come back, so if he wanted one of the daggers to be his, he had to take immediate action. He put the letter about the Smithsonian employee in his OUT box so it could be delivered in the interoffice mail on Monday. That ought to be soon enough.

He took a deep breath to clear away the fatigue. He felt a sort of catch in his chest. Odd! It was an unfamiliar though not particularly alarming feeling. He looked down and there was something on his shirtfront. In the fading light from the window it appeared to be steel and stuck out about half an inch, like a long, thin, sharp shirt stud. It looked, in fact, like the end of a government-issue paper knife. It was getting red around where it came out of his shirt. It got to be time to take another breath and he realized with growing panic that he wasn't going to be able to do it.

A butane lighter flared briefly above the late Victorian settee in the darkest corner of the room and in a moment a wisp of cigarette smoke drifted to where Dr. Kraft lay across his desk. Dr. Kraft ordinarily didn't like cigarette smoke but this time he didn't notice. His murderer sat waiting patiently. It would be a while before Dr. Kraft quit dripping. In a bit, his murderer wandered quietly down the hall toward the big supply cabinet next to the Xerox room. The cabinet was well stocked. It served, after all, the Secretary's office and those of the Treasurer and several of the Assistant Secretaries. Of course it contained a roll of fresh blotting paper. Dr. Kraft would have seen to that or at least Olive would have. Oh, yes, and a large manila envelope. That would do nicely.

After a second cigarette the murderer decided it was time

to move Dr. Kraft. There was very little blood and what there was had been caught nicely by the desk blotter. The murderer cut up that blotter neatly and enclosed the pieces in the manila envelope. In block letters, the murderer addressed the envelope to the Internal Revenue Service in Philadelphia, and then hunted around in Olive's desk for some postage stamps. There weren't enough, so it would arrive "postage due." If the IRS accepted it, the murderer decided, the envelope would be found to contain blood-soaked paper. That couldn't be an uncommon occurrence at IRS, so it would simply be burnt. If the IRS refused to accept it, it would become the Postal Service's problem since there was no return address. The murderer smiled at the thought, and put the fresh sheet of blotting paper in the leather-edged holder. The murderer looked around the office. There were two cigarette butts in the rarely used ashtray. The janitors would clean those out on Sunday night or if they didn't, Olive would blame them for it.

Satisfied, the murderer proceeded with the other arrangements. Everything was going exactly according to plan, but there was much still to be done.

 *Two*

It was early in July, a month earlier than Dr. Kraft's un-heralded return to Washington, that the telephone buzzed on Henry's desk. He hunted for it among the piles of file folders and other papers. The cord was there so the phone had to be somewhere. He pulled on the cord and Greece, Guatemala, Guinea, and Guyana slid off the desk and into the wastebasket. The telephone stood revealed, the intercom button illuminated. He lifted the receiver.

"Hello?" he said rather irritably.

"Mr. Scruggs? There's a call for you." The temporary recep-tionist hung up without saying who was calling.

"That's one we won't keep," Henry muttered into his dead telephone, and punched the blinking button on line 5091. "Hello," he asked rather tentatively.

"Mr. Scruggs? Mr. Kraft wants to see you." No explana-tions. That was typical of her, Henry thought. And Olive, Dr. Kraft's secretary, never asked, she ordered. She was also an inverted snob. It was *Mister* Kraft, not *Doctor* Kraft, because his was an academic doctorate.

"I suppose I can spare him a few minutes this afternoon. Tell him to come on over now, if he likes."

"Here."

"Beg pardon?"

"Here. Over here. People come to see Mr. Kraft; he doesn't go to see them." Olive let her voice harden enough for Henry to understand that it would be silly to argue the matter and that he had already exceeded her patience. What little she had.

"When?" Henry capitulated.

"Now. He's waiting for you." Olive hung up.

She's another one I wouldn't keep, Henry thought. He picked up the cup of tepid tea from its safe haven in his OUT box, drank it down, and got to his feet. He looked out his small, arched window at the carousel on the Mall. It was spinning around and around, going nowhere. He wished he were on it, going nowhere, instead of going to Assistant Secretary Kraft's office. He could hear the sound of the carousel's calliope music coming through the closed windows in the air-conditioned tower of the Arts and Industries Building (called by one and all, the A&I). He hated calliope music. It was impossible not to march in cadence with the calliope when you walked across the Mall. Musical tyranny. It made you look silly, something like a wooden carousel horse.

Henry looked ruefully down at the files in his wastebasket. The country file for Greece had landed inside-out and a decade of papers that nobody had bothered to punch and fasten down had spilled out, some in the can and some out. An overclassified *SECRET* State Department telegram lay face-up. A line from the Broadway musical, *The Prettiest Girl in the World,* came to mind. "We're up to here in Greece." Henry still held his State Department top-secret clearance, but averted his eyes from the secret document anyway. No need to know.

"I'm going over to Dr. Kraft's office," he said to the expendable temporary, who had gone back to reading her paperback antebellum Gothic, and he began to descend the sixty-two steps that led down from the tower and into the underground tunnel joining the A&I with the Smithsonian Institution's Castle.

Henry had been working for many weeks on a summary of

the thousands of things done abroad by the Smithsonian Institution, or under its sponsorship. It was Henry's own fault, of course. When he had come over from the State Department six months earlier to be a liaison officer (for want of a better word—Henry was actually hiding out from the State Department while he looked for a job elsewhere), he had asked lots of people what the Smithsonian was up to abroad. Nobody had been able to answer that, of course, which was not really surprising since nobody, no one person, knew what the Smithsonian was up to domestically either. All the five-hundred–odd scientists, scholars, and other program people did more or less what they wanted to and often didn't tell even their department chairmen what was going on.

So when Ambassador (retired) Craddock had asked Henry what he wanted to do, Henry right away suggested doing a compendium of overseas research and exchanges. Ambassador Craddock had loved the idea. He, like Henry, had served his term at diplomacy and was a bit at a loss for something useful to do at the Smithsonian besides double-dip on his State Department retirement pay.

The real reason Smithsonian Secretary Harlan Whitfield had hired Ambassador Craddock to run the Smithsonian's Foreign Affairs Office (FAO) was that it looked good to have an ex-ambassador guiding the Smithsonian's international activities. "Guiding," of course, was the wrong word. Nobody guided anything at the Smithsonian. "Blessing" was the better term.

Craddock had been a career man at State, not a political appointee, and had risen to the top and been appointed ambassador to the Unicorn Islands Confederation, the least-important country in the world. This ambassadorial assignment crowned his career and had come to him only after he had successfully completed a mission as U.S. representative (with personal rank of Minister) to the World Congress on Migratory Kites.

As it happened, the Smithsonian's Division of Fishes had enjoyed several seasons in the Unicorn Islands identifying fish in local fish markets under a grant from the United Nations' Food and Agriculture Office, and kites were of particular interest to the Chairman of the Division of Birds. So Craddock's meager and purely diplomatic qualifications in the twin fields of fish and birds were taken as fitting him admirably to head up foreign affairs at the Smithsonian.

July was the slow season. All the scholars who could dig up travel money were out in the field digging up whatever. All, that is, except for a few who normally worked in places where the summer months were too hot. And, of course, Assistant Secretary Kraft, who had delayed his departure because he didn't dare miss Secretary Whitfield's politically vital Fourth of July party.

At this time of the year there was hardly anything that FAO had to do to get travelers through foreign ports of entry and to track down lost equipment shipments.

But it was also the season when somebody was very likely to drown abroad or be captured by natives and have his head shrunk. Not that the latter had happened recently. Henry had wondered, idly, whether in such a case the body could be returned to Washington for half fare. If it were possible, the accounting division would insist on it. He could imagine the trouble it would be to redeem the other half of the ticket cost from some foreign air carrier. On the whole, he would prefer that the unfortunate would drown and the remains be eaten by sharks. It should then be easy enough to get the whole return fare refunded—"reasons beyond the traveler's control." When he undertook his next great project, writing the definitive handbook on the undertaking of foreign research, he would have a whole chapter on the subject. "Taking Advantage of Excursion Rates and Other Savings on Foreign Air Travel" came to him as a possible chapter title.

While Henry and the other members of the FAO staff stayed behind waiting for whatever catastrophe ill-chance might provide, Ambassador Craddock had gone on vacation to Bermuda to play a bit of golf and spend at least one of his dips.

And Henry worked on the Compendium in defiance of

Assistant Secretary Kraft. Last winter when the Compendium idea had first come up somebody had mentioned it to Dr. Kraft, who had summarily forbidden it. "I won't have you bothering my scientists! If you have to know what's going on, just have lunch with the bureau directors. They'll tell you all you need to know." That had irritated Craddock and had assured Henry's project.

"Watch it, Henry!"

He almost collided with Mrs. Wiggins, who was on her way up the narrow, switchback stairs carrying her lunch. Mrs. Wiggins usually shopped during her lunch hour and brought back something to eat later during office hours. Henry could see the point of the resulting two-hour lunch but he valued his food too much to accept anything that came in Saran Wrap. "Kraft called. He wants to see me."

"Tell him 'uh-uh, no way,' " she said to Henry sternly. "He shoulda thought about his fuckin' passport when he switched from Federal to th' Trust Fund." Sally Wiggins was proud of her street-talk and was fully prepared to use it against any whitey, including Assistant Secretary Kraft. Not just poor Henry. It was not generally known that she was solidly middle class and had gone to a Catholic girls' college, albeit within a city bus ride from Harlem.

Henry was in a bad position because he knew that Sally was right. She usually was. It wasn't that she was a legal expert; she just had unerring instincts about these things. If you wanted to do something, there had to be some sort of a rule against it. It was a principle that had seldom failed her.

If Kraft had been smart, he would have told Sally that now that he had switched from the Federal Civil Service to the Smithsonian's Trust Fund, or private, side, he never wanted to see his red official passport again. Then Sally would have found a reason why he couldn't use a blue tourist passport but had to use the official one.

It was a curious and often tedious situation, the Smithsonian Institution being both in government and out of it. Partly funded by the Congress and partly supported by private funds. Partly staffed by civil servants and partly by private employees. No one quite knows what the Smithsonian is, and the Institution tries to take advantage of the confusion by assuming the advantages of both worlds.

In modern times, nothing was more revealing of this confusion than the way the State Department's Passport Office had treated Smithsonian employees. For much of the time since passports came into general use in the twentieth century, the State Department had issued official passports to all Smithsonian travelers, whether they were members of the Civil Service or not.

Unlike the ordinary tourist passports, these official passports identified the holders as being representatives of the government of the United States. In some cases, indeed most cases, such travelers received unusual courtesies from customs and immigration officers in foreign countries. Holding such a passport also could mean the waiver of visa fees, unusual consideration from foreign police, and other advantages. But occasionally it worked against the traveler, where foreign countries had their own reasons for being inhospitable to our government representatives.

But by the time of this story, a minor brouhaha involving a Smithsonian scientist in North Africa had caused the official passport entitlement of Smithsonian employees to be reexamined. The matter even received Congressional attention and the then director of the Passport Office, the formidable and congressionally well-connected Frances Knight, had handed down a dictum. No more official passports for Smithsonian employees regardless of rank unless they were paid by appropriated funds and were required to take a federal oath of office.

Perfectly clear? Well, not really. The Secretary of the Smithsonian continued to be issued official passports. And he was paid from private funds and he took no federal oath of office. But the Secretary's position was established by Act of Congress. So he could be an exception? Well, perhaps, but certain other Smithsonian positions, lesser ones, were established by Act of Congress as well. And those Smithsonian officials were denied official passports.

The State Department and the Smithsonian dealt with the quandary by not thinking about it. In the interest of keeping the peace with the Smithsonian Secretary, everybody hoped the matter would never come up.

Everybody but one, that is. Assistant Secretary Kraft wanted an official passport. To wear as a fig leaf for his ego. And he was prepared to do whatever was necessary to get it.

However, Dr. Kraft had given this little (if any) thought when a year earlier he had switched from federal to trust. Presumably, he switched because he liked the private "trust" retirement system better. That and it made him hopping mad those times when the Congress was late with the appropriation and all the feds had to take leave without pay.

When Dr. Kraft's old official passport expired and he had apply for a new one, he demanded another official one. And he wasn't about to take "No" from a Harlem black woman who wore T-shirts emblazoned with anti-establishment slogans—*UP YOURS TOO; BLACK BY POPULAR DEMAND; IF YOU CAN READ THIS YOU'RE NOT CLOSE ENOUGH; THERE ARE MOTHERS AND THEN THERE ARE MOTHERS; HONK IF YOU HATE HONKIES.*

Kraft wasn't going to like taking "No" from Henry either. Henry might be white, but he was just a State Department gofer. And, he was Tennessee hillbilly. Can you imagine that? What a combination! No wonder they can't do anything right!

62, 61, 60, 59—Henry counted down the sixty-two steps from his office in the A&I tower, putting Dr. Kraft out of his mind and paying attention to more immediate concerns. At the foot of the stairs, a tunnel led out of the A&I and to the basement of the Smithsonian Castle a short distance to the west.

The tunnel was low enough so you just naturally tipped your head at an angle to keep from bumping it against the fluorescent lights and conduits fastened to the century-old brick arched ceiling. The top of the tunnel came so close to

13

the surface that you could feel the July heat baking the ground a few inches above your head. A bald head, particularly. Henry stretched his stride and counted out thirty-three paces.

He always hurried through the tunnel because he was convinced that one day it would cave in from the weight of the tourists crowding the space between the A&I and the Castle. As an asthmatic, Henry had an abiding fear of smothering. A half left turn and two paces more before he felt the relief of the tunnel opening up for a half flight of ascending steps.

Henry avoided the ancient, creaking, malevolent elevator in the east end of the Castle and instead took the stairs. It meant a delay of three minutes after passing Mr. Taggart at the guard's desk on the main floor. He always had to exchange a word or two with Mr. Taggart. To do less would be rude, like treating Taggart as though he wore a guard's uniform instead of his black funeral suit.

"Good afternoon, Professor." Mr. Taggart always called Henry "Professor" for some reason. Henry supposed it was because he had looked blank the first and only time Taggart had tried the "How about those Redskins" gambit. Taggart was not one to repeat his mistakes.

Today the tourists, weather, and vacation were all touched upon lightly as safe conversational subjects. The weather: hot. The tourists: Where do they all come from? Vacation: Saving mine for winter when it's too cold to get out of bed. Henry looked at his watch as he moved on. Barely over two minutes. Faster than the elevator even when it didn't get stuck and smother him to death. He climbed the steps two at a time—*2, 4, 6, 8,* the landing, *10, 12*—.

"You certainly took your time, Mr. Scruggs. He's busy now. You'll have to wait."

Henry stood for a moment, breathing heavily. He looked expectantly at Olive, but when it became apparent she wasn't going to ask him to sit, he looked around and found a chair and sat down defiantly. He was wheezing slightly. No

14

pollen in midsummer, it must be the dust in the Castle or maybe it was Olive. He certainly could be allergic to her.

The chair was ugly and Victorian. It was too low, so his raised knees pushed his back against the carved woodwork which dug into his spine. It would have been more comfortable to stand, but he stayed with the chair resolutely. Olive ignored him but there was a slight smile on her face. She had to know what the chair felt like.

"Okay, you can go in now." She said it without looking up, having apparently decided he had suffered enough.

Without thinking, he tried to rise from the chair in the normal way. It was disastrous. Pushing with both feet simply caused the chair to penetrate his back deeper. He finally managed to roll out of the chair sideways and land on his knees. That was what she had in mind, Henry was sure of it. She wanted him to come to her boss on his knees. Damn her. Damn him.

When Henry made it to his feet, Kraft was standing there in the doorway, dressed in his cool blue shirt sleeves with those stupid white cuffs and collar. Stupid little buttons held his collar down as though it might otherwise fly away. A chaste and narrow (and secretive) dark tie hung from the stupid collar. By now, Henry was sweating and his tie had gotten outside his jacket. He was sure the points of his collar were sticking straight up, but he wasn't going to feel them to see. So much for his dignity, Henry would just have to prevail with the strength of his reason alone.

"Come in Henry," Kraft said condescendingly. "I'm having a little problem with a member of your staff," Kraft began. "Mrs. Wiggins, is it? She is trying to take away my official passport. Can you imagine?" He gave Henry a look that momentarily suffered him to share Kraft's milieu as long as he remained acquiescent. "I'm sure she thinks she is just trying to do her job but she's being unnecessarily bureaucratic. I asked you to come over because I'm sure that between ourselves we can straighten this out." Kraft looked challengingly at Henry. This in itself was unusual because in

15

the many times they had met before, Kraft had always ignored him completely.

"I was aware of your application, Dr. Kraft. Unfortunately, Sally has no choice. When you had your job converted to the Trust Fund, it clearly made you ineligible for an official passport."

"Goddamn it, I'm telling you to find a way!" Kraft abandoned his thin effort at conciliation.

"An official passport isn't always an advantage. It makes it more difficult to get into East Europe and Spain, and—"

"I don't want to hear all of that! I know the arguments. Nobody goes to East Europe if they can help it. The hotels are lousy. When I travel abroad I represent the Smithsonian. It's an official agency—"

"Quasi," interjected Henry.

Kraft looked at Henry impatiently. "Well, maybe it's quasi-official to you, but foreign governments regard us as official and how do you think it looks if I'm being met by some cabinet minister and I have to pull out one of those tourist passports?"

"Well, it looks the same as it would if you were president of Harvard, or maybe General Motors." Henry knew as soon as he said it that there was no point in arguing, but he went on, tediously explaining the law and Mrs. Knight's policy regarding official passports.

"Frances Knight? Good heavens, man! She's been gone for years. Get a new ruling, Goddamn it! If you're good for anything you ought to be able to get your friends over in the State Department to give a little on this."

"I've talked to them. They're still afraid of Mrs. Knight. They refuse to reverse it."

"Well, make it an official Smithsonian request. Send it to the Secretary of State, for Christ's sake. Tell him that Secretary Whitfield has an official passport and he's Trust Fund, just like I am!"

"That's exactly the problem. If we raise the question officially, the secretary might lose his own official passport. When the subject came up years ago, it appears everybody

16

danced around the Secretary's status. His position is unique, but in some respects akin to that of a member of the Cabinet.

"We seem to have continued to request official passports for him in spite of Mrs. Knight's ruling and nobody at State has questioned it. If we try to extend the official passport to the Assistant Secretary level, it's likely they would say 'No' for all Trust Fund people. We might even lose official passports for the federal Smithsonian employees as well even though they are under Civil Service."

"I don't see why—"

"In the years since the ruling by Mrs. Knight, our General Counsel has gone to considerable effort to establish that the Smithsonian is not an executive agency in the normal sense, and that we are not bound by Executive Orders, though we generally choose to comply with such orders voluntarily. It's likely that such reasoning would be found to be in conflict with the federal regulation that limits official passports to 'officers or employees of the U.S. Government.' "

"Lord deliver me from amateur lawyers! Scruggs, you're still with the Goddamned State Department, aren't you?"

"Yes, sir, but I'm on loan to you, to the Smithsonian. I'm really on your side, it's just that this is something I can't change." Henry smiled sweetly at Dr. Kraft. He was beginning to enjoy himself.

"You may mean well, which I doubt, but you're just one of those pettifogging cookie-pushers at heart. No wonder the U.S. is in such a fucking mess abroad. I want to see an official request, prepared for the Secretary's signature, on my desk tomorrow! I'm traveling to India and Ceylon the end of next week and you're going to have to hustle to get it straightened out." Kraft turned back to the papers on his desk and ignored Henry.

Henry sighed, his enjoyment shortlived, and left by the door opening directly into the hall. That way he avoided Olive in the next room. He was sure she had listened in on the intercom. She would have found a way to twist the knife, demanding that Henry submit a draft of the request for her review, or something like that.

Henry counted the sixty-two steps back up to his office. At the top he was puffing. He had to start taking better care of himself. He leaned on the railing at the top to catch his breath.

"Scruggs, did you sell us out?" Sally demanded to know.

"No, at least I don't think so. He insists I prepare a letter from Secretary Whitfield to the Secretary of State. I'll do it, but I'll recommend the Secretary not sign it."

"Kraft will have your ass for that."

"Yeah, probably."

Henry was late leaving the office. It didn't take too long to draft the letter Kraft wanted, but the memo to Secretary Whitfield took much longer. It had many Xeroxed attachments. Henry carried the letter to Kraft's office. Everybody was gone, so he bypassed Olive's desk and left it in the middle of Kraft's desk blotter. He then walked across the hall where he found Miss Norton, the Secretary's overworked staff director, still at her desk. He left the memo with her and departed. The memo was marked for the Secretary's attention only and went into detail as to why sending the letter would not be a good idea.

"Ambassador Scruggs!"

Henry didn't have to look around to identify the voice. Only Hamilton Sealyham called him ambassador, just as only Mr. Taggart called him professor. Hamilton was Director of Conferences, a unit of the University Programs Office, which put on, as one might expect, conferences.

"If I ever become an ambassador, Hamilton, what will you call me then?"

"I don't know, my dear chap, perhaps Mr. Secretary. I always try to look to the future. Isn't it late for you to be here? Surely this is the cocktail hour."

"Hamilton, it is late and this has been a tiresome day. I have been beset with Mr. Kraft."

"Our own John Armour Kraft, Jack Armstrong, the all-American Assistant Secretary?"

"The same."

"Henry, he besets everybody who's anybody and a large number of those who aren't. I'm surprised he's just getting around to you. I think he was sent to us to try us on earth as a condition to our entry into heaven, if there is such a place. Of course it also renders purgatory unnecessary and is part of the Congress' simplification act."

"I thought that was only for paperwork simplification."

"Oh, my dear chap, it is. That's all purgatory ever was. I can't imagine what else you'd call paperwork."

Henry changed his mind about the cocktail hour. "Right now I think Mr. Kraft has established my eligibility for entry into the bar at the Hotel Washington. Could I buy you a drink?"

"What a nice idea! Why didn't I think of that? Do allow me to call my wife and tell her I'll be delayed."

"She won't mind?"

"Heavens no! It will give her a chance to meet her young man, if she has one." Hamilton stepped into an empty office to use the telephone.

Henry decided not to pursue that one further. In a couple of minutes, after an amicable phone call, Hamilton was ready to go.

"You must understand, Henry," Hamilton said after they were comfortably settled at a small table in the Hotel Washington bar and Henry had explained about the day's problems, "Kraft is one of the three original palace eunuchs who came to the Smithsonian from California with Secretary Whitfield."

"Eunuchs? I don't see how the term applies. Is it a sexual reference?"

"Not at all! I mean it doesn't say anything about their sexuality, one way or the other, though they are from California, whatever that may mean." Hamilton rolled his eyes significantly, but significant of what, Henry couldn't be sure. "Eunuch used here simply means that they could be and

19

were indeed given seemingly limitless power by the Secretary, but that they could also be counted on to do his bidding, whatever he might ask. A bit like having free run of the harem without, ah, you know—"

"That certainly wasn't my impression of Kraft. He seemed only too ready to screw things up for the Secretary."

"Exactly so! We have seen demonstrated here that, contrary to what is commonly supposed, castration is reversible. In this respect, at least. It is also true with the other eunuchs."

"Who are they?"

"Why, Percy, of course, is the most infamous. Percy Jammers, my own superior, limited to the hierarchal sense, obviously. As you may know, my conferences receive no official funds—"

"You mean no federal funds?"

"I mean no Smithsonian funds of any kind."

"How do you, uh, do things?" asked Henry, quite willing to be led away from what he thought was the subject.

"I have to raise everything outside. I have to go hat in hand all over the country to find money to support things that should be funded by the Smithsonian. Things I might add that have traditionally been supported by the Institution in former and happier times."

"I thought the Office of University Programs got a lot of money?"

"They do, they do! A scandalous amount! But that's all frittered away on Percy's pet projects. Nothing comes to me! Nothing!" Hamilton rotated his empty glass with his fingers and looked at it dolefully.

"How does Jammers get by with it?" asked Henry.

"That's just it, dear chap! Percy gets away with it because the Secretary has given him unlimited power, and of course he reports to Jack Armstrong—"

"Kraft."

"Yes, Kraft, if you wish, who supports him completely."

"Why don't you go directly to the Secretary?" Henry swallowed the last of his drink and set the glass down with a louder than necessary thump.

"Lord knows, I've tried!" Hamilton stared at Henry's glass with gathering cheerful melancholy. "Your glass is empty. Waitress, another round, please, we're in desperate straits over here! Now where was I? Oh, yes, going to the Secretary—he is always sympathetic of course, and says he'll try to do something in the next budget round, but after Kraft and Percy get to him, nothing ever happens."

"You said there were three," Henry reminded Hamilton. "But nobody else controls your budget, do they?"

"Why, of course! Don't forget the Treasurer. Our Dillard Haley. He is always there. Like the monkey in Le Fanu's *Green Tea.*"

"I don't see—he doesn't really get into the budget process, does he?"

"How little you know about the Smithsonian's quaint ways, coming as you do from a proper government department! The Treasurer does all manner of things to defeat me. For example, when I get a grant from a foundation, he demands twenty-seven percent for what he calls 'overhead,' despite the fact the Smithsonian places all the responsibility for accounting and everything on me! Kraft and Percy cut out all my travel money so I have to scrape up what I need from outside. Haley demands his twenty-seven percent of the travel money as well! If I am offered a plane ticket, I have to beg for extra money to pay the Smithsonian so I can accept it. It is immoral! It is extortion!"

"It sounds like three retirements may be the only solution," observed Henry.

"Well, of course! But the eunuchs are all younger than I am! Perhaps they might meet with accidents. Accidents are no respecters of youth, nor should they be! Formalin in the water cooler, hot oil carelessly dropped from the great tower—that sort of thing." Hamilton drummed his fingers on the table a moment, staring into the middle distance. "No, I suppose that the Smithsonian might draw the line at that, though it does seem at times to tolerate behavior just as questionable. However, I am not without my resources."

Hamilton waited until the drinks were delivered and then continued: "Where they made their mistake is that they have offended and ill used more than just myself. I am of course as nothing. Nothing at all!" Hamilton's false modesty gushed softly over the table for an instant and was then gone, as though it had never been.

Henry spoke up hurriedly. "I hardly think that Kraft's insistence this afternoon on an official fig leaf amounted to a capital crime."

"No, no, yours was nothing—yet— I'm talking about grievous, even egregious, offenses. For example, our friend Taylor—Taylor Maidstone, I mean—has had the same sort of problem with Kraft. He came here from the University of Chicago with a written understanding that the Smithsonian would fund his anthropological film-making program. It was a critically important point because films gobble up money much faster than do my poor conferences. Kraft keeps reducing Taylor's budget to force him to resign.

"It is now to the point that he gets only office expenses and has to fill out his staff with hopeful volunteers. All of the anthropological films he makes are paid for by grant money or gifts from individuals. And, on top of all that, there is still the Smithsonian extortion for twenty-seven percent! Dillard's so-called overhead. That large a percentage levied against what it costs to make a film is what I believe is called 'big bucks'!

"Taylor and I are supporting the rest of the Smithsonian as well as our own activities. It's really too much! If people are going to come to us for money like we are the government, we should be given the authority to tax!" Hamilton's voice rose in outrage and he gulped down the remainder of his drink.

"Why doesn't Maidstone go to the Secretary about it?"

"He has, he has. Many times. The Secretary keeps telling him to put his needs in his annual budget request and Kraft keeps knocking his request back out of the budget."

"I suppose," said Henry, "that I really have no cause to complain about my little problems with Kraft."

"Nobody ever has just little problems with Kraft. You've crossed him now and that has raised your profile. And you needn't think that he won't see your little confidential memo to the Secretary. He is certain to do something really nasty to you. Expect it and prepare for it."

"I'll come to you and Taylor for consolation."

"To us, and there are others too. You will not lack friends. Both halves of anthropology hate him. Physical anthropology people think he starves them in favor of the archeologists and the archeologists think physical anthropologists get everything."

"Which ones are right?"

"They both are. He diverts funds from both sides to support his own pets. He does the same throughout the Museum of Natural History, playing one department off against another. The only people who seem to like him are those at the zoo. That's only because they are so far away from the Mall and I suppose if they get hungry enough they can eat their animals."

"Is the arts side of the Smithsonian as bad as this?"

"In some ways it is even worse, since arts curators are totally without conscience, but I like to think that Assistant Secretary Vernon is not as venal as Kraft and Company. Women are biologically more nurturing, and Lylene's womanhood seems to have survived her years as an arts curator. Kraft, on the other hand was suckled by a wolf. Or perhaps a lizard—no, I don't suppose that's anatomically possible."

"I suppose Kraft makes Percy look pretty good by comparison?"

"No! Of course not! Percy has control of all the predoctoral and postdoctoral fellows. The departments depend on the doctoral fellows for doing all the dirty work nobody else wants to do. Nobody feels fairly treated by Percy, not even the zoo!"

"You know, Hamilton, when I got the State Department to lend me to the Smithsonian, I thought this was going to be such a nice place. I thought that it would be full of people who were here because they really enjoyed what they were doing. It seems I was completely wrong. It's just like the State Department or anyplace else."

"No, dear friend! You had it exactly right. The professionals, at least, are here because the Smithsonian is one of the few places they can do exactly what it is they want to do. Things would be wonderful but for an accident that occurred when we were establishing our collections."

"I don't understand."

"Well, as you know, even with our collections totaling more than sixty-two million* objects, it is simply impossible to have complete collections of every conceivable type."

"Yes, I've noticed some surprising gaps."

"Just so. The diversity of collections reflects both the market availability of objects and the past interests of our curatorial staff. For instance, we are weak on Egyptian Pharaonic arts and crafts, but very strong on mummies. But the case in point is our Byzantine collection. Very poor in pots and pieces of buildings, but the Smithsonian has accessioned, in spirit, the justly famous administrative style of a Byzantine court, rich with devious and duplicitous detail."

"I would have said," said Henry, "that it was more of a feudal system, with the museum directors as landed nobles having fealty to King Harlan Whitfield in his castle. Perhaps the Assistant Secretaries are the landed bishops."

"No, no, dear boy! That is an interesting analogy, but it is based only on appearances. The reality of it is much more obscure, with many overlapping power systems weaving intricate arabesqueries. That is why Whitfield and his cronies

---

*At the time (1970), the Smithsonian thought its collections comprised about sixty-two million objects. After an intensive program of inventorying and computerization of the collections, the number at present (twenty-two years later) is known to be more than double that. The true number of objects in 1970 was probably about a hundred million.

may well not prevail. Other forces, some active and some now sleeping, can be drawn upon. And I shall certainly do so!" For the first time that evening, Hamilton appeared to smile. Henry was reluctant to ask him why he did so.

 **Three**

"Ah, Miss Claridge, I was wondering—" Henry paused. He was finding it difficult to go on.

"You better call me Janie, Mr. Scruggs. The other sounds like you-know-what." Janie giggled without embarrassment.

Henry wasn't sure he could, but he was determined to give it a try. Janie was all curves and maybe nineteen. She looked like one of the girls in those old *Esquire* cartoons, without the jading experience. A middle-aged man's pick-me-up.

"Janie—" There, he said it and it was relatively painless though he was sure he could never get used to it. Perhaps she would accept "Jane" when she knew him better—"I was wondering whether you would like to go out with me?"

"Gee! I don't know! I mean—" Now Janie looked embarrassed and she would have frowned except that her skin wouldn't wrinkle. The inside ends of her eyebrows climbed slightly. She groped for an excuse.

"I mean for lunch," Henry said hastily. He wanted to avoid outright rejection, if possible. If she started to balk at the lunch invitation, Henry was prepared to say he meant lunch in the Commons. The Commons was the staff dining room in the far end of the Smithsonian Castle, and going there could hardly be construed as a date at all.

"I guess that would be all right." Even Janie with her

vestigial perceptions realized she wasn't being very gracious. She felt clarification was necessary. "It's just that Temposec tells us we're not supposed to date the men. Particularly—" Janie ran out of words. Henry took it to mean that she particularly wasn't to go out with dirty old men who wanted to take her to bed. That included 90 percent of the males over age twelve. Maybe eleven. And the other 10 percent were, well—and her father, Henry added the thought, to be charitable.

"I had in mind our going to the Mayflower Hotel." Janie gasped involuntarily. Henry plunged on. "It has a very good restaurant.

"But we can go somewhere else if you like. Some people don't like hotel dining rooms." He offered that when, after a pause, it became apparent she wanted a way out.

They settled on Hammel's. It was close to the Mall and the food was good if you could ever get served. Everybody saw them leaving and knowing looks bounced off of them like rice at a wedding.

Every day for weeks the temperature had climbed into the upper nineties. The afternoon rainstorms that had provided a cool-down at sundown from late June and through to the big storm on the final day of the Smithsonian's Folklike Festival, July 6th, when the big Siouan council tepee blew down out on the Mall in front of the Smithsonian Castle taking with it most of the feathers from Chief Bended Elbow's ancestral headdress, had now given way to the drier heat of midsummer. Dry heat in Washington means a humidity of about 85 percent.

What little wind there was rattled the heat-dried leaves of the big border elms, and the grass on the Mall had already begun to scorch. Henry and Janie's feet kicked up dry dust as they crossed to the north side. They were not quite arm-in-arm. To be accurate, they walked at arm's length, with Henry lagging slightly behind so he could watch Janie's behind out of the corner of his eye. Janie kept her eyes down as if looking for lost nickels and dimes. She didn't find any. You never do on the Mall, though Henry had once found a New York City subway token.

The tables at Hammel's were so close together that intimate conversation was just about impossible. Anyway, Janie concentrated on her lunch to the exclusion of practically everything else. She put ketchup on her french fries and ordered a drink with an umbrella. That came as a shock. Henry had forgotten what it was like to be nineteen. That is, if he had ever known. He decided it didn't really matter and gave his full attention to his own plate of cold poached fresh salmon hollandaise. It was delicious.

Henry toyed with the idea of devising a written test for all future candidates, but the list of questions was too long and it seemed unlikely that any of the Tempos could fill out the questionnaire without help and that would skew the results. He resigned himself to enjoying the other pleasures of summer in Washington. The pollen count had gone down as the temperature had gone up and he had not had to take an antihistamine since early June. Assistant Secretary Kraft had finally left on his trip to India and Ceylon, without the protection of an official passport, and with any kind of luck he would be attacked and devoured by a Great Indian Bustard. Ambassador Craddock had fallen off of a motor scooter in Bermuda (doubtless while ogling young girls) and was having to take an extra two weeks to recuperate from unknown injuries. All was right with the world, albeit a lonely world.

Janie really liked desserts. That almost made up for the ketchup. She and Henry became quite chummy over chocolate mousse cake with rocky road ice cream. But it was like your baby daughter's birthday party. Henry returned to the office feeling older and lonelier than ever.

Since his return from Switzerland almost three years earlier and until coming to the Smithsonian, Henry had spent most of his time at Green Pastures. For those who don't already know, Green Pastures was the underground and only fitting name for the Atomic Energy Commission headquarters out in Germantown, Maryland, housed as it was in a building of fine early post-Armageddon architecture with massive, atomic-blast-resistant walls facing Washington 35 miles away, interior partitions designed to blow down harmlessly and be reerected with minimum fuss after an atomic blast, and deep buried fallout shelters with their self-contained water and power supplies. Well-tended rolling green lawns gave this cynical refuge of eternal life in the post-atomic hereafter the look of idealized tranquillity.

First the AEC and now the Smithsonian. Henry seemed to be making a career of being assigned to other agencies. Or, to put it more precisely, he was unmaking his career by being assigned outside of the State Department. He thought of himself as a remittance man, like those nineteenth-century Englishmen who were embarrassments to their families and were paid an allowance, a remittance, as long as they stayed in some distant British colony. Australia was very popular for remittance men. British Honduras worked almost as well.

What was wrong was that Henry had made no particular friends. At least, not the sort you'd go bowling with. (Henry would not be caught dead bowling. Imagine what a bowling ball could do to your hand if your thumb got stuck in it!) Anyway, at AEC the leisure-time sport had been guns. All the real AEC men shot big-bore pistols and stuck empty .38 cartridge cases in their ears to protect themselves from the noise. It looked very he-man to have bullets sticking out of the sides of your head. They wore NRA shooter's hats and looks of unnatural calm.

After he came over to the Smithsonian (thus avoiding an assignment to Australia that would not have saved his career though it might have postponed his demise from the Foreign Service), Henry felt that going shooting with the boys somehow seemed inappropriate. Nobody at the Smithsonian except the guards shot at anything. No, that wasn't quite right. Dr. Kraft shot endangered species of birds out of their nests and the people at the zoo all the time were shooting tranquillizer darts at things. For whatever reasons, Henry was more or less without friends.

There was Hamilton Sealyham, of course, but Hamilton was really just a good acquaintance. The same and perhaps less could be said for Ronald Hipster, the assistant director of Henry's office. There was nothing really wrong with Ronald, Henry supposed, except that he was quite mad. Not that that necessarily disqualifies a friend if he has other qualities, which Ronald did not. Gerald Blackman, the other Foreign Affairs Officer, hardly counted. He didn't do anything but work and you well can imagine how dull that was.

Besides, what was really wrong with Hamilton, Ronald, and Gerald was that they simply weren't girls. Henry really liked girls and not for just the obvious reasons. Girls were fundamentally more interesting. Except when they were stupid, of course. One stupid person is pretty much like another and the sex hardly matters.

He had thought about having an office romance, but his attempt to initiate one with Miss Claridge had been very disheartening. Anyway, she was gone within a week and another girl from Temposec had taken her place. The new one, Miss Deeds, chain-smoked. Besides, even if you could stand her cigarettes, there was something that looked like an engagement ring on her finger.

Now that he thought about it, the most interesting Temposec had been Mrs. Phyff, a lady in her early fifties who had passed through the FAO in early June. She had refused to take Henry's overtures seriously. After she had earned all the money she felt she needed, she quit the Smithsonian and Temposec and went on an around-the-world cruise on a freighter. Or perhaps several freighters—Henry wasn't sure.

So that only left the permanent staff ladies of the office, and there were only two of those—Sally Wiggins and Dreamy Weekes. Sally's husband was a construction worker who apparently didn't get tired enough on the job so he spent his spare time doing what they call "working out," which Sally described as lifting heavy pieces of iron that made dents in the floor when he lowered them. Then, she complained, he was too tired to do things like carry out the garbage or run the vacuum. She seemed to like him anyway.

He was kind of a big ball of muscle, which was all right because so was Sally. Henry was not about to tangle with either of them.

Dreamy Weekes was an entirely different matter. Dreamy ran the Smithsonian's Special Foreign Currency Program. From the moment Henry joined the office she had flirted with him shamelessly. He had been beguiled at first by her attentions but lately was coming to the reluctant realization that it was just her way. It was nothing personal.

She had a bond of sorts with Henry because he had seen her passport and knew that her real name was Dora, a fact she closely guarded. She had been called Dreamy since she got out of diapers and it had strongly influenced her life. She had become an outrageous tease. She had a husband, too, but it was an on-again off-again marriage and anybody could see why.

The other thing about Dreamy was that she was apparently telepathic. She knew immediately when Henry had given up on the nubile temporaries and was sniffing after her. She was delighted.

So one day Dreamy was sitting on a stool out in the big central room of the FAO offices sorting through her grant proposals. She was all legs and arms stuck together by a minimal bit of clothing in the middle. She ordinarily fiddled with her grant proposals in her own office in September, which was plenty of time for the late October advisory council meetings. There was really no point in sending proposals out for peer review while all the university professors and researchers were out making it with their graduate students.

She had positioned her stool where Henry couldn't help seeing her if he looked out his office door. For a long time he looked at her out of the corner of his right (his best) eye, around the edge of the frames of his glasses. Henry had so much astigmatism that he couldn't see Dreamy as sharply as he would have liked to, but he wasn't about to turn his head enough to look through the upper part of his bifocals.

Henry watched Dreamy. Dreamy watched Henry watching her. Or so she thought. She was almost sure. Actually, her own eyes weren't that good and she was far too vain to wear glasses. She was nearsighted and wouldn't have needed glasses in the office except for watching Henry. And when she was out and about she felt didn't really need them for distance either since she didn't much care about identifying trees from the shapes of their leaves and things like that.

So she had a pair of glasses but never wore them. Her husband told her that was the reason why she had piled her car into a traffic signal pole last winter. That had nothing to do with it, she had explained. Her attention had been distracted by a dude in a Lincoln. That wasn't so (though it well might have been) but she had said that just to upset her husband. Which it did.

Now, while keeping her eye on Henry, Dreamy arched her back like a stretching cat and did something totally scandalous and outrageous. Henry couldn't believe his eyes, imperfect though they might be. He quit making any pretense of working on the foreign research profile and concentrated on Dreamy, squinting his right eye to see her more clearly. As anybody who's a photographer knows, when you squint it's like closing down on a lens aperture. It cuts down on the effects of lens imperfections. You always see paintings of Indians squinting into the distance. That's because they never had glasses and wouldn't have worn them if they had because it wouldn't have looked sufficiently warlike.

Dreamy did it again. Now Henry was convinced. She really had done it. Slowly and without moving his head, Henry reached down and slid open the right hand lower drawer of his desk and groped for his Leica. It was mounted with his Summarex 85-mm lens. It was very fast for an old lens. Pretending to be working, he put the Leica on his desk, hidden behind a stack of files—Sudan, Surinam, Swaziland, Sweden, Switzerland, Syria, and Tanzania.

Carefully, he estimated the distance—18 feet—and the light—$f2$ at 1/60th. No, he'd better open up the Summarex all the way, to $f1.5$ because Dreamy had dark skin and the shadows would block up. Then he pointed the camera at Dreamy and waited. Damn! He almost forgot to cock the

double-stroke film-advance lever. There! Now he was ready.
Henry pretended to ignore Dreamy until she couldn't
stand it. She looked around the office to see whether anybody else was watching (that was Henry's signal to get ready)
and then she repeated her horribly vulgar and even obscene
gesture, worse than before. With his left arm Henry swept
the files from in front of his camera and with his right
forefinger he pressed the shutter release.

Dreamy didn't hear the shutter release. Leicas are very
quiet. But what she saw was the Summarex's huge objective
lens. Even without her glasses it was unmistakable. In one
bound she came flying through Henry's office door and
lunged across his desk. Files flew everywhere. Henry
clutched his Leica to his bosom, behind his crossed arms.

Now it was unfortunate that Henry was ticklish. Otherwise
there might have been no confusion and all would have
understood that he was being assaulted by Dreamy. As it was,
he and Dreamy collapsed in a giggling heap in the narrow
space between the desk and the bookcase behind his chair.
The chair, itself, was now in two sections that had gone their
separate ways. Only Dreamy's behind loomed significantly
above the desk when viewed from the door.

"Here, here, I say!" Ambassador Craddock pounded one
of his crutches against the frame of Henry's office door.
"What's going on here?" That was a silly question because it
was perfectly clear what was going on, more or less.

Henry and Dreamy tried to get up but they were wedged
in tightly in the narrow space. "Could you help us, sir?
Maybe you could pull the desk toward you?"

Craddock could not. He could barely stand. He advanced
haltingly into the room and started beating on the desk with
the crutch. Several blows landed on Dreamy's posterior.
"Goddamnit, Craddock, stop it!" she yelled. In short order
the rest of the staff crowded into the office and Gerald and
Sally had the presence of mind to pull out the desk. Henry
and Dreamy carefully untangled themselves.

"Scruggs? Mrs. Weeks?" Craddock sputtered and drew
back to take another swing with his crutch, but Sally caught

hold of it so it wasn't going anywhere. "What the hell have you two been doing?" he demanded.

"We thought you wouldn't be back until Monday," Dreamy said defensively.

"Obviously."

"Well, it's Henry's fault. He took my picture." Dreamy looked all pouty.

"That wasn't any reason for you to attack me." Henry had both hands busy rewinding the last few frames back into the cassette.

"Of course it was. You didn't ask for permission."

"You would have refused."

"Of course I would have refused. That's not the point. You were supposed to ask."

"That's just the same as saying nobody's allowed to take your picture. Anything you do in a public place is fair game!"

"This isn't a public place!"

"It is, too. Ambassador Craddock, sir, isn't our office a public place?"

"God help me! Scruggs, give her the film and get this place cleaned up. And quit behaving like children. I ought to fire you both but I don't think I could describe what you were doing on the personnel action."

Henry finally negotiated just to open his camera and spoil the exposed part of the film that was outside the cassette. Dreamy was not pleased with that, but agreed because Ambassador Craddock appeared to be dangerously upset.

"How is your leg, sir?" she asked as he limped from the room. She had decided it was time for a little solicitude.

"It hurts. And you two don't make it any better!"

"Poor baby," she said.

Henry was content. The exposed negative of Dreamy in disgrace was rolled safely in his cassette. Henry would print up lots of copies and leave one for her to find in her desk so she would know he had her in his power. She would do whatever he demanded.

Henry would say this for Dreamy, she stayed after the close

of business (it would be inaccurate to say "after work") to help Henry get his scattered papers back into the proper files. Henry used the time to good advantage. He invited Dreamy to go for the weekend with him to Ocean City.

"I don't have any need for a suntan, Henry honey." She was laughing at him. He had the sort of skin that would peel off like a snake's if he spent the day on the beach.

"I didn't have in mind going out very much."

"Well, I'll let you know. I'll have to ask my husband."

An hour or two in the darkroom and Henry would change that! Or so he might have believed had he not known Dreamy so well.

Four

"You don't have to explain, I know about the IIE." Henry did indeed know about the Institute for International Exchanges. It was the bane of his existence. The State Department's Bureau of Educational and Cultural Affairs (CU) invited all sorts of foreigners to visit the United States and IIE was one of the principal organizations making the arrangements.

They were always suggesting that the foreigners visit the Smithsonian. That would have been fine if they were content with the part of the Smithsonian every tourist sees. But IIE always wanted some sort of official, behind-the-scenes tour. The curators, researchers, and other specialists generally hated these visits. They used up endless time and accomplished nothing. Secretary Harlan Whitfield generally refused to see anybody unless the visitor were royalty or something like that.

Since nobody wanted to see the visitors, it fell to Henry and his colleagues in the Foreign Affairs Office to entertain them. He might just possibly have been glad to have received a visitor over the past endless weekend because Dreamy had turned down his offer of a trip to the beach. But now that Monday had finally arrived, Henry had far better things to do than make conversation with some foreign official who was bored with the Smithsonian or who wanted something (such as money) that was an impossibility.

The voice on the phone shifted gears, moving on past his set piece about IIE and on to the subject of the visit. *"Dr. Sabuki would like to see Secretary Whitfield to pay a courtesy call."*

"Well, I'm not sure the Secretary will be available," said Henry, allowing his voice to express his profound doubts.

"Only for a few moments, of course. Dr. Sabuki met him when the Secretary was studying snails in the Republic of Cape Royal. About fifteen years ago."

"Republic of Cape Royal?"

"Yes. That's where Dr. Sabuki is from. If Secretary Whitfield isn't available, perhaps Dr. Sabuki would settle for Assistant Secretary Kraft."

"Kraft is out murdering birds in Ceylon."

"Murdering birds?"

"Yes. He left here with two shotguns, four cases of shells filled with number six shot, and an untold number of body bags."

"Body bags?"

"Yes, plastic bags for the casualties. It sounds awful, doesn't it? But it's better than usual. Kraft usually spends the summer in London murdering our travel budget. Says he's looking at the fallen in the British Museum. He'll be back week after next when the travel budget runs out. Maybe your Dr. Sabuki would like to look at our medical history exhibits. I could probably get a docent to take him through. Sometimes there are a few docents left in town this time of year."

"I don't think he's really interested in medical history, but he would like to see your Physical Anthropology Department. He's keen on foreign sicks—or something, I think he said."

"Forensics, probably," said Henry. It began to look a bit more possible, though much of Anthropology's professional staff was out of town doing research, seducing graduate students, and things like that. "I'll see if I can find somebody in Physical Anthropology to talk to him. I'll also check the Secretary's office and call you back as soon as I can."

* * *

On Wednesday morning, Henry struggled up the steps to his office by nine forty-five. He had remembered as he sat down to what was intended to be a leisurely breakfast that Dr. Sabuki was due in his office at nine-thirty. Henry had turned off his tea kettle, drunk his orange juice, abandoned the rest to his resident mouse, and left his house at a dead run.

Dr. Sabuki was already sitting by Henry's desk. Henry mumbled his apologies while he put on the tea kettle. "I thought we might settle down here and talk about the Smithsonian for a few minutes before we get started with your tour." Henry desperately wanted his tea.

"Now, what can I tell you?" Henry asked rhetorically as he served up their tea. He knew exactly what he could tell Dr. Sabuki; he had been through this dozens of times before. The story had little to do with what the Smithsonian was today, but Henry found it much more interesting that a recitation of facts about the Institution.

"The Smithsonian is a trust instrumentality of the United States, not quite private, but certainly not a part of the government." That meant precisely nothing to Dr. Sabuki, who sat there at polite attention, not quite yet bored.

"The Smithsonian was founded one hundred and twenty-four years ago, in 1846, by Act of the American Congress, but it had its roots in English society of the eighteenth century.

"In the eighteenth century there was an Englishman, Hugh Smithson, who came from a long line of haberdashers who had managed to work their way up to the minor title of Baronet. Hugh was a Fourth Baronet in 1740 when he married the rich Lady Elizabeth Seymour. Lady Elizabeth had the wherewithal to buy her husband the title of First Duke of Northumberland of the Third Creation."

"I don't understand this 'Third Creation,' " said Dr. Sabuki. "I know of course what barons and duke are."

"I'm not surprised. It only makes sense to the English. In England, when a ducal family line dies out, Parliament can re-create the dukedom with the same name for another family. I believe the Percy family were created the original

Dukes of Northumberland in the fourteenth century. They endured until Bloody Mary executed the last Duke in the mid-sixteenth century.

"The Dukedom of Northumberland was later created again, but the Second Creation died out in the seventeenth century. The Lady Elizabeth Seymour that Hugh Smithson married was a descendant of the Percy line and Hugh was therefore able to apply for the name and arms of Percy through the Third Creation. So you see, he became the First Duke, but of the Third Creation.

"Hugh, as Duke of Northumberland, became a Lord of the Bedchamber to King George II, among a number of other honors hallowed in British tradition. Hugh then took as his mistress a wealthy London widow, Elizabeth Macie, who was a niece of Charles the Proud, Duke of Somerset, and who claimed to descend from King Henry VII.

"Four illegitimate children blessed Hugh's dalliance with Elizabeth Macie: James, a younger brother Henry, and two sisters. I don't know what happened to the sisters. It is only the brothers, James and Henry, who concern the Smithsonian.

"James Macie was born in 1765. He was educated at Pembroke College, Oxford. When he reached his majority, he took his father's surname and thus became James Smithson. He was born in his own twenty-first year, so to speak. Because of his illegitimacy, however, James was cut off socially from his upwardly mobile father. There were other, presumably legitimate, heirs to Hugh, however, and the title of Duke of Northumberland of the Third Creation thrives unto today.

"James lived on the Continent much of his life as an expatriate, and pursued a career in science. He traveled extensively in Europe, where he came to know the leading scientists of his day. He had many scholarly papers published by the Royal Society of London, of which he was a member. It is said that among his scientific papers, was one devoted to a chemical analysis of a lady's tear. Reflecting, I like to think, the unfortunate plight of his two sisters, his brother, and himself.

"James never married and near the end of his life, he prepared his will in which he left his fortune to the United States of America, as residuary legatee, "to found in Washington, under the name of the Smithsonian Institution, an establishment for the increase and diffusion of knowledge among men." No one is quite certain why Smithson made such a bequest to a country he had never visited and whose form of government he appears never to have advocated.

"There was some suggestion that he was mad. Others have speculated that the wording of his will regarding the 'increase and diffusion of knowledge' might have been drawn from the speeches of George Washington. Washington used somewhat similar wording in his speeches, which were circulating in France at the time Smithson traveled there."

"And what about his brother Henry?" asked Dr. Sabuki. He had been paying attention after all.

"Henry did, apparently, marry. Or at any rate, he produced a son. It was this son, James's nephew, who was the primary beneficiary of James's will. But upon James Smithson's death, in Genoa, Italy, in 1829, the nephew inherited only a life interest in the considerable estate. He could only draw upon its income, not upon the principal."

"I understand the distinction," said Dr. Sabuki, a bit impatiently.

"The will provided that if this nephew, at that time a twenty-nine-year-old bachelor, should die without an heir, the principal of the estate should come to the United States of America, to establish the Smithsonian.

"The nephew did indeed die in 1835, and without issue, and the estate, valued at more that half a million dollars, in one hundred and five bags of gold sovereigns, came to the United States. It was this money and the conditions set forth in the bequest that founded the Smithsonian," said Henry.

"That is the Smithsonian endowment? Is that the right word?" asked Dr. Sabuki.

"It is the right word, but the story of the Smithsonian's

endowment is not without its complications. At the direction of Congress, the money was turned over to the Treasury with the instruction that it be invested in state bonds.

"Now comes upon the scene Mr. W. W. Corcoran, the extraordinary Washington broker. In the mid-1840s, Mr. Corcoran sold millions of dollars' worth of United States bonds abroad to finance the Mexican War. Some years later, in the 1860s, during the American Civil War, Corcoran, who was a Southern sympathizer, found it expedient to get out of Washington and move to Paris, where some believe he sold a considerable amount of Confederate bonds to help finance the war. He had to be doing something in Paris besides playing with his grandchildren.

"I don't know how familiar you are with our Civil War," said Henry, who was fully prepared to digress to China if the occasion were presented, "but the Southern tier of states seceded from the Union—"

"Yes, I know. It was about slavery. Many of my relatives were involved, I suppose, in a manner of speaking," said Mr. Sabuki.

"I shouldn't be at all surprised. Though slavery was by no means the only issue." Henry looked at his watch. It was getting late and he didn't believe there would be time to go into the Southern viewpoint of the War Between the States. He returned to the beginnings of the Smithsonian.

"In 1838, before either of these extraordinary bond sales efforts, Corcoran was promoting American state bonds. He sold a half million dollars in these state bonds, mostly State of Arkansas bonds, to the Treasury for the Smithsonian account.

"Perhaps foretelling the unfortunate fate of the Confederate bonds more than twenty years later, the Smithsonian's state bonds in a short time largely defaulted, wiping out the Smithsonian's endowment. I'm sure that Mr. Corcoran felt considerable sorrow on this account. He was a cultured man and, indeed, founded the excellent art museum in Washington that bears his name. You should see it before you leave town.

"He was also charitable to those less fortunate than he and founded an old-age home for impecunious Southern gentlewomen, women said by some to have been his cast-off mistresses. That was something Hugh would likely have approved." Dr. Sabuki had finished his second cup of tea and was beginning to fidget. Henry saw he was losing his audience. He poured some more, now tepid, tea into Dr. Sabuki's cup. That should hold him long enough to finish his spiel.

"After much argument in Congress and the consuming efforts of one of our former presidents, John Quincy Adams, who was then in his old age a congressman from Massachusetts and Chairman of the Select Committee on the Smithson Bequest, the money was replaced by the Congress and in 1846 the Smithsonian Institution was born. Son to James, grandson to Hugh, and in a manner of speaking a lineal descendant of King Henry VII.

"Considering the huge amount of money available, there were many proposals for the use of the Smithson bequest. Setting aside less worthy proposals, Congress established the Smithsonian as a separate, virtually autonomous institution, under the guidance of a Board of Regents drawn from all of the branches of the national government and from the private sector, and under the immediate administration of the Secretary of the Board of Regents, known best as the Secretary of the Smithsonian.

"Princeton professor and eminent scientist Joseph Henry was chosen as the first Secretary of the Smithsonian. Henry, and the eight other secretaries who have followed him, have created the largest, as well as the most diverse and complex, museum-based nongovernmental research and educational institution of any place or time. Today, there is no institution quite like it or better known in the world.

"Today, the Smithsonian encompasses about a dozen museums (not all of them yet open), a zoological garden, a major astrophysical research center, a tropical research institute, and many other research facilities of varying degrees of permanence. Its staff exceeds three thousand and its annual budget considerably exceeds a hundred million dollars, making its seminal endowment of half a million seem rather small."

"Now, I think we should move on to the Museum of Natural History," he suggested. Dr. Sabuki? *Dr. Sabuki!*" he called somewhat louder.

Dr. Sabuki woke up with a start and the teacup slipped off his lap and onto the floor. "Very interesting," he said, just in case something particular had been said to him. "And will I be able to see Secretary Whitfield? That was my principal reason for coming to the Smithsonian."

"I regret that the Secretary is out of the country at the moment," lied Henry. "I thought you might like to see our Physical Anthropology Department. We're doing some very interesting things."

"Perhaps, then, could I have a meeting with your Dr. Kraft? We have corresponded for years."

"You are an ornithologist?" Nobody had said anything about that. Henry could have arranged a visit to the Bird Division if he had known.

"No, we collect beer coasters. I began my collection while I was studying in England. I have them from all over the world."

A rare, human side of Dr. Kraft, if trivial, thought Henry. "I explained to the man at IIE that Dr. Kraft is doing research in Ceylon. I'm sorry if you expected to see him while you are here."

"They said nothing to me. Well, what is it, then, that you have to show me?"

Henry walked with Dr. Sabuki across the Mall toward the Museum of Natural History. Henry was doing his best not to walk in cadence with the calliope. He tried to walk three beats against two, but that was too quick and Dr. Sabuki was falling behind. He reversed it to two beats against three and found his visitor was getting ahead of him. Finally, he capitulated and marched along with Dr. Sabuki, the calliope, and everybody else on the Mall. He chattered more about Smithsonian history as he went. There seemed little likelihood that Dr. Sabuki could fall asleep while they were walking.

"The Castle, behind us, was our first building and dates from just before the Civil War, with construction beginning about 1847 and continuing through the mid-1850s. Workers in 1865 burned much of the roof by accident. They connected a stove to a flue that didn't lead into a chimney. It could have happened to anybody." Dr. Sabuki nodded uncomprehendingly. They didn't use chimneys in Cape Royal. "The Castle was designed by James Renwick, an American architect who also built Grace Church and St. Patrick's Cathedral in New York and at least three other buildings in Washington. Renwick is said to have modeled our Castle after the ancestral Norman Romanesque revival castle of the Dukes of Northumberland.

"That's a statue of our first Secretary, Joseph Henry. There, to our left, with the pigeon decorating it. Secretary Henry asked for a building of modest proportions and the Castle was what he got—a red stone building in a city where public buildings were white stone, a vertical building in a low, mostly horizontal city, and a determinedly asymmetrical building in a city dominated by classical symmetry. A few later buildings followed the Castle's precedents, but not many.

"The Arts and Industries Building, behind us, was completed in 1881 to house the collections gathered for the 1876 American Centennial Exposition in Philadelphia. As you can see, it is a much less somber building than the Castle. Instead of dark, crenelated stone, it is built of red brick and colored grazed brick accents and has a symmetrical design and a light structure making use of iron columns and trusses.

"The Natural History Museum, ahead of us, is our first twentieth-century building and dates from 1911. The wings on either side were added in the 1960s. Beyond the trees, ahead and to our left, is the Museum of History and Technology which opened in 1964. Behind and to our left is the Freer Gallery, dating from 1923 and housing collections of

Near East and Asian art and some turn-of-the-century paintings, most importantly, those of James McNeill Whistler.

"The white marble building to our right and across Seventh Street is the National Gallery of Art, built just before World War II. It is an autonomous museum, part of the Smithsonian system but administered separately." Dr. Sabuki, now wide awake, looked with interest everywhere that Henry pointed. Henry often wondered if foreign visitors paid any attention to the things he said. Sometimes he felt he was just elevator music, intended to be soothing noise and nothing more.

Henry didn't notice Secretary Whitfield until it was too late. They almost collided on the Natural History Museum steps. Lamentably, Dr. Sabuki recognized the Secretary at once. "Ah, Mr. Secretary! How nice! I had so hoped to see you!"

Henry jumped in with both feet. "Mr. Secretary! I'm happy to see you back so soon! I had just explained to Dr. Sabuki that you were away from Washington and wouldn't be able to see him."

Secretary Whitfield recovered quickly. He had, in fact, been spending the afternoon in his snail laboratory, attending to business of the Universal Gastropoda Society, of which he was international president. It was a long tradition of Smithsonian secretaries that they continued their research and other scholarly activities while acting as Secretary to the Smithsonian Board of Regents and, as such, being chief executive officer of the Smithsonian. As President of UGS, Secretary Whitfield was general editor of *Inter Nos Gastropoda,* the Society's occasional publication of learned papers about snails and other such creatures.

"Yes, the meetings were cut short and I'm back in town early. Why don't you bring Mr. uh—"

"Sabuki, Dr. Sabuki," supplied Henry.

"Uh, yes, bring the doctor over to my office about four-thirty. We can talk for a few minutes about—"

"Cape Royal," added Henry.

"Indeed! I remember Cape Royal very well!" Secretary

Whitfield could say that safely. He had been everywhere and Cape Royal could be no exception.

But Dr. Sabuki was an intelligent chap and couldn't have been fooled Henry thought, as they climbed the wide cascade of steps leading up to the door of the museum. He supposed that the same sort of thing happened all the time in Cape Royal. He appreciated Dr. Sabuki's good manners.

They were a bit late getting to the Physical Anthropology laboratory. Henry had talked too much on the Mall and then there had been the encounter with the Secretary. And now Dr. Sabuki had to be gotten a temporary badge and Henry was too polite to push ahead of the crowd of tourists at the reception desk in the rotunda where the badges were issued.

Then there was the problem of getting to the Anthropology lab in the east wing. When the new east and west wings were added to the old central building in the Sixties, the ceiling heights were quite different. Consequently, it was possible to walk down a corridor on the old building third floor and suddenly find yourself on the fifth floor of the wing.

Henry got hopelessly lost several times. With Dr. Sabuki in tow, he turned into one corridor only to find tables of dead rats on all sides and stretching into the distance. A mouse-faced technician was bending over a table making notes. Henry was horrified; Dr. Sabuki was fascinated. Henry dragged him away to an area covered with dried grass and asked for directions. A kind-hearted botanist led them to the proper office. Dr. Sabuki's regard for Henry must have been considerably eroded, but his polite demeanor was unchanged.

Dr. Hans Christian Fabricius, a Danish postdoctoral fellow, was the only professional available. Everybody else was out in the field looking for bones and such (and, as previously noted, the flesh of young female anthropology students). Dr. Fabricius specialized in the Bronze Age cultures of the deserts of the Middle East where it was too hot to work this time of year, so he was in the cool of the air-conditioned laboratory playing with his favorite toy, his computer. It was an odd piece of equipment, largely homemade but tied into the Smithsonian's new mainframe computer system.

Dr. Sabuki nodded politely but uncomprehendingly while Hans explained how he used the computer to map underground shaft tombs by measuring the electrical conductivity of the desert sands. Moisture collecting around buried masonry of the tombs lowered electrical resistance between electrodes placed in a grid upon the sand, locating the tombs with remarkable precision. Then Hans moved on to tell how the computer and a digital scanner worked together to create records of the museum's huge collections of bones for the collections inventory.

Dr. Sabuki immediately perked up. "We have many bones," he said, "in our natural history museum. We put accessions numbers on them, as I suppose you do, but it is almost impossible to compare one bone with another. A skull is a skull, so to speak."

"With the computer, a scanner, and our inventory language, no two bones are alike," Hans boasted. "I will show you how it works!" Hans went down a long aisle and opened a collections storage box at random. He pulled out a shelf and carried it and the skeleton it contained back to his computer workstation.

"You see, we place the skull in the illuminated box. The skull is suspended so it can be rotated for scanning from all sides." Hans turned on his computer and booted up the inventory program. Then he pressed a button which made the scanner sweep across the front of the box. He repeated the process with the skull turned to show the sides, back, top, and bottom. With each sweep, the computer screen briefly filled with symbols. Then Hans typed in a *CLASSIFY* command and the computer set to work sorting out the scanner data.

"Eventually, we will have everything set up so the operations can be done automatically. Right now, we can only take a series of static views of the skull. But with machine manipulation of the skull, we will be able to program the scanner to make a much more precise dynamic mapping of the skull's contours. Only a single technician will be needed to keep a dozen terminals running and we can put the whole anthropology collection into the data bank in four or five years. Presuming, of course, that there is enough storage room in the main computer. As it is, we have only a small portion of our collections, less than five percent, in the data bank which we have entered during the course of the development and testing of the system."

The computer completed what it was doing and a menu appeared on the screen. Hans punched *STORE*. "Might as well enter this one since it's been scanned." The machine went back to work and the phrase *FILING DATA* appeared on the screen. "As well as automating the scanning, we expect eventually to have faster computer chips so that the processing time can be cut down considerably."

The machine beeped at them and the phrase *DATA ALREADY ON FILE* appeared on the screen. "It seems we've done that one already. Whoever did it should have marked it."

"Is that all your computer does? Just describe the bone?" asked Dr. Sabuki. "Our records have not so much physical information as data about where the bones are found and how old they are."

Hans punched in a command and a form appeared on the computer screen. "One step which I omitted was filling out this form. I was going to do it later because the information will have to come from the old accession record card in the Registrar's office. However, since this specimen is already in the machine, I will call up the record for you." Hans typed *ACCESSIONS DATA* on the keyboard.

The computer was quiet a moment and then the record appeared on the screen:

> IDENTIFICATION OF SPECIMEN: SKULL,
> JAMES SMITHSON, ENGLISHMAN.
> SEX: MALE
> AGE: BORN 1765, DIED 1829
> LOCATION: RECOVERED FROM ENGLISH
> CEMETERY, GENOA, ITALY

DISCOVERED BY: ALEXANDER GRAHAM
BELL, 1904
ACQUIRED BY SMITHSONIAN 1904 BY GIFT
[SEE MINUTES OF THE BOARD OF REGENTS
MEETING, OCTOBER, 1904, AND MEMORAN-
DUM OF THURSDAY, NOVEMBER 3, 1904,
FROM SECRETARY LANGLEY TO THE DIREC-
TOR, U.S. NATIONAL MUSEUM.]

They stood there, shocked, looking at the screen. "This is a joke," suggested Henry after a few moments.

"I hope so," said Hans. "Some people like to play with the computer." He picked up the skull and looked at the accessions number, then he picked up the telephone and dialed. "Hello, this is Hans in Physical Anthropology. I wonder, could you check an accessions number for me?" He read the number off of the skull and waited a few minutes. "Uh-huh, are you sure?" There was a short time during which the voice on the telephone was raised so the others could actually hear it albeit indistinctly. "Yes, I know you don't make that kind of mistake, but I have a reason for asking. Well, thank you, as always."

Hans hung up the phone. "It is Mr. Smithson," he said.

Mr. Sabuki looked puzzled. "This isn't the Mr. Smithson who founded the Smithsonian?"

"He never came to America except as a set of bones. These bones, apparently."

"And his bones were just put in the collections of your museum? Why did they—"

"Go to the trouble for just another set of old bones?"

"Well, yes. In my country we don't particularly worship the dead but we would at least keep the bones of such an important man in a tomb."

"That's where Smithson is supposed to be—in a sarcophagus, in the crypt next to the Great Hall in the Castle," explained Henry.

"I wonder," asked Hans, "who is in the sarcophagus?"

Five

"I am delighted to meet you, Mr., ah—" said Secretary Whitfield graciously.

"Dr. Sabuki," provided Henry dutifully.

"Sabuki," agreed Dr. Sabuki. "We so much enjoyed having you visit our country in 1960, wasn't it?"

"Yes, that's it exactly, 1960. I remember it very well."

"No, it couldn't have been," Dr. Sabuki decided, "it must have been 1955, because I had just gotten my assistant professorship."

"If you say so," said Secretary Whitfield, growing a bit confused. "I believe I was collecting your snails." That was a safe guess because Whitfield was always collecting snails.

"Yes, indeed," said Dr. Sabuki looking pleased that the Secretary remembered his trip. "You visited our university, Rifi-Fifi National University, and saw our collections. Then, of course, there was your lecture. It is still talked about. Among the older members of the staff, of course. The average age of our faculty is twenty-six."

Secretary Whitfield was silent while he tried to imagine such a thing. Henry moved into the silence. "Mr. Secretary, we have been taking a look at the research being done in Physical Anthropology on the computer data bank."

"Yes, indeed!" That was something he liked to talk about.

It was one of the areas of Smithsonian science not resting peacefully in the nineteenth century. "We have a very large collection of human skeletons and within a few years, we expect to be able to do all of our comparative studies by computer. I may decide to give up snails!" Whitfield laughed heartily at his little joke and after a moment, Henry and Dr. Sabuki joined in. "It will be a long time before we will have snail skeletons on the computer," said Whitfield, just to be sure his guests had gotten it.

"Your Dr. Fabricius gave us a demonstration," said Sabuki. "It was most curious. Evidently the bones of your founder, Mr. Smithson, are over in the collections of your natural history museum. The computer recognized them right away."

The Secretary suddenly gave them his full attention. He looked at Henry for an explanation.

"That's right, Mr. Secretary, the computer identified Smithson's skull. We also checked the accessions number on the skull through the Registrar's office. It is Smithson, all right."

"But it's not—have you tried to find out how it got there?" Whitfield demanded.

"We only found out an hour ago that it was there. Dr. Mayes is supposed to be back in his office on Monday. We thought we'd start with him."

Another weekend. It was too hot to go anywhere, so Henry stayed at home, wearing shorts and a T-shirt. He considered going naked but when he tried it, it felt funny. He tried going barefoot but since he spent most of his time playing his piano, the pedals hurt his feet and he put on leather sandals. He didn't like that either so he kicked them off and moved over to the harpsichord. It had no foot pedals.

The harpsichord had been a mistake. He had bought it when he lived in Vienna and it had seemed wonderful. Finally, he would be able to play early music and have it sound the way it should. He could tune it himself so he would never have to put up with a tuner's fanciful ideas of well-tempering. It was light enough so it wouldn't make furrows in the floor when you moved it. And it was beautiful—graceful and delicate.

The reality of the harpsichord was something else. When Henry adjusted the little leather quills, or plectra, so they plucked the strings evenly, the touch of the keyboard was uneven. If he adjusted them to make the keyboard even, some strings plucked loud and others soft. That was intolerable. So he accepted the uneven keyboard and adjusted for even sound. That made those keys that were hard to press down have a delay and those that were easy, plucked immediately. His playing sounded ragged and irregular. He hated it.

Nevertheless, on a hot day he could at least tune and temper the instrument and play it until he lost his patience with the keyboard. Henry sat down and removed the music rack. Then shifted the keyboard to the eight-foot strings, the strings with pitches corresponding to those of a piano. He then struck his tuning fork on the top of his bald head and held the stem of the fork against the harpsichord's sound board. While the fork rang a 440 concert pitch A, he struck A on the harpsichord. It sounded at about a high G flat. Since the last tuning, the air conditioner had dried out the harpsichord and shrunk the wood, lowering the tension on all the strings.

Henry took his wrench and moved the 1A string up to A and tuned the As in all the other octaves to match. Then he tuned the rest of the eight-foot strings to their approximate values, and shifted in the four-foot strings (tuned an octave higher) and brought them up to pitch. This would increase the tension on the harpsichord frame so that the real fine-tuning could begin. There was no point in fine-tuning part of the scale of the instrument if other keys had to be pulled up to pitch.

Once everything was more or less tuned to the proper pitch, Henry used the tuning fork to tune a true A. Then he concentrated on a single octave, tuning fourths and fifths, expanding the fourths and contracting the fifths by about a

52

beat per second to achieve well-tempering so that the player could shift from one key signature to another without retuning the instrument. The well-tempered octave was the hardest part. Once achieved, the rest of the keyboard could be tuned relative to the octave, with only a bit of checking, especially at the extremes of the keyboard, to be sure that the tempering remained true throughout.

Almost two hours later, Henry decided he had it right. He tried the Bach Italian Concerto and made it most of the way through the first movement. He decided he hated the harpsichord every bit as much as he remembered, and went and fixed a drink. Scotch was just as good as he had remembered it.

On Monday morning, Emeritus Senior Physical Anthropologist Dr. O. Arlington Mayes smiled as Henry and Hans Christian Fabricius invaded his office on the third floor and north side of the rotunda of the Natural History Museum. Dr. Mayes got to his feet to welcome them. He was a very courtly man, lean and gray and dressed as always, even in August, in a dark pinstripe vested suit. He looked for all the world like a country doctor. He was, in fact, one of the first American physical anthropologists to take a medical degree.

"How did your field trip go? Did you find anything interesting?" asked Henry.

He looked blankly at Henry.

"Weren't you doing field research this summer?"

"My research? I researched rainbow trout. They were biting far too frequently for my taste."

"Oh, I thought—"

"Oh, I don't hunt for bones anymore. Except in my fish. Doesn't do to swallow them, though a little mashed potato always seems to take care of the occasional accident. I leave the scrabbling about to those eager youngsters who like that sort of thing. One of the advantages to being emeritus. I have in my time collected all the human remains I will ever be able to study. Why look for more?"

"We have found a skull that might possibly interest you," said Hans, getting right to the point.

Dr. Mayes showed a flicker of curiosity. "Let me see it," he said.

"We don't have it here. It's down in the collections," said Hans. "It seems to have belonged to James Smithson."

"He was a mineralogist. And a chemist. I don't believe I ever heard that he studied physical anthropology, though I suppose—"

"It belonged to him in the sense that he was born with it," Henry explained.

"Oh!" They now had Dr. Mayes's full attention.

"Yes, it should be in the crypt. Mr. Scruggs brought over a foreign visitor and I thought I would demonstrate our new computer and scanner setup." Hans described just how he had tested the skull.

"There were *The Corsican Brothers,* or was it *The Man in the Iron Mask*—anyway, what about twins?" Henry asked.

"Impossible," said Hans, "we've checked twins. The odds against identical skulls are astronomical."

"Quite right," said Dr. Mayes, but he radiated interest. It pushed back the grayness that usually dominated his appearance. He glowed. "A few years back," he began, "the crypt over in the Castle was redecorated. It hadn't been redone since Alexander Graham Bell and some of his friends brought Smithson's bones back from the English Cemetery in Genoa at the turn of the century. I think it was 1904, though I'm not certain because, despite appearances, I wasn't around at the time."

Dr. Mayes occasionally jested about his age. Nobody else would have dared. "The Italians had been about to dig up the section of the cemetery where Smithson's grave was located. Well, the fellows got the bones back but they couldn't be a hundred percent sure they had the right bones. Anything could have happened in the seventy-odd years the body had been buried.

"The science of forensics has come a long way in this century, and when we had to move the bones out to redo the crypt a few years ago, we brought them over to the department to have another look at them. We talked it over and decided it might now be possible to reconstruct the physiognomy of Smithson from the skull and to compare it with the surviving life portrait of Smithson."

"Did Hrudlicka study the bones when they first arrived at the Smithsonian?" asked Hans.

"I wondered about that. You know Hrudlicka was my teacher. But there is nothing in the records about it and I never heard him say. Of course it would have happened years before I arrived.

"Anyway, the bones were disinterred from the sarcophagus and brought over to our department and I set about modeling Smithson's head. We carefully made two casts of the skull and put away the original. The first cast we used for reference, and then we took the second cast and started adding clay, using the standard tissue depths that have been determined from thousands of measurements," he explained for the benefit of Henry.

"What was the result? Was it Smithson?"

"I felt that the results were inconclusive. So much depended on the painting's fidelity that in my opinion we could not give a definitive answer. But neither could we rule out the skull being Smithson's. The more compelling evidence was of course metaphysical."

"Metaphysical? I don't understand."

"The Smithson bones have always been accorded almost mystical regard. In fact, the power of these bones was said by some to account for the most remarkable fact about the Secretaries of the Smithsonian Institution.

"In this century, between the time the bones arrived and the time we moved the bones out of the Castle, Smithsonian Secretaries almost never died, even though they usually received their appointments when well into middle age. There had been only six Secretaries during this stretch of more than seventy years. Only two of those had died. Powerful magic! Of course the two who died, Secretaries Langley and Walcott, apparently weren't protected, but Langley was already ill when the bones came. I don't know what went wrong with Walcott. Lost faith, probably.

"However, during the short time while the bones were outside of their regular resting place—the crypt—Secretaries seem to have lost the protection of the bones and two more of the former Secretaries died. The only ones who survived were the sitting Secretary and the one former Secretary, Dr. Callaway, who came in to do his research every day in the Anthropology Department. There are those who say that the sitting Secretary survived because he had authority over the temporary resting place of the bones and Callaway because of the proximity of his laboratory to the bones."

"What do you believe?"

"It doesn't matter what I believe. What matters is that I don't disbelieve." Mayes looked thoughtful for a moment. "Dr. Fabricius, I suppose it is a silly question to ask, but you are certain it was the actual skull you found and not the cast? I made a very good cast."

"There is no doubt, Dr. Mayes. It was too light for a cast. And a skull has its own feel. I can't describe it."

"I know what you mean. Anyway, the cast should be down in my laboratory, so that can be checked if necessary. Now for the computer record—I recall letting someone use the cast to enter the data into the bank. And so it matches the real one! I am pleased to have the quality of my work confirmed by your wonderful machine. Odd that old Smithson should be back in Anthropology. I supervised his return to the sarcophagus myself."

"We should do something," suggested Henry.

"Indeed we should! I think the first thing we must do is to be sure former Secretary Callaway has his will in order. He said he was going to leave some of his money to the Anthropology Department and since he doesn't come in to work in the building anymore, he may have lost his protection."

Henry phoned Secretary Whitfield about his meeting with Dr. Mayes and the Secretary asked him to prepare a memo on it. The Secretary liked having disagreeable things put on paper so they could be delegated more easily to somebody else. Hans helped with the technical part of the memo and Henry got him to sign it as a joint memo. Henry had learned to share the blame for disagreeable things whenever possible.

Under Secretary Rossmore Owens convened the meeting on Smithson's bones. Owens was an experienced, long-time bureaucrat highly skilled in dealing with other peoples' headaches. He was good at his craft because he generally avoided becoming personally involved. That is, he maintained his objectivity and was not really concerned with what the solution was just so long as the problem went away. He surveyed the conference table and assessed the problem. His secretary had as usual engaged in overkill. He would have been happier dealing just with this fellow from Foreign Affairs, Henry Scruggs. Scruggs would have to do what he was told or he could just be sent back to the State Department.

A few years ago, when Owens had first arrived at the Smithsonian, Doris, his secretary, had left someone important out of a meeting. It had been a bad day and he had fussed at her more than he should. Thereafter she had always invited everybody who could conceivably be involved. Now this was just a case of museum artifacts and they were not missing but had turned up in the wrong place. Oh, well, let's begin. Odd group of people. Dare he speak to Doris about it again? No telling how she might take it.

"Good afternoon, Miss Casey, and, ah, gentlemen. You all received copies of this memo on the holy relics?"

Everybody nodded. Indeed, Henry and Hans had written the thing. Miss Casey spoke up. "The General Counsel would have come but he seems to be away and Mr. Bodde—"

"Couldn't be bothered," supplied Owens.

"Uh—" Phoebe Casey looked flustered. "He was busy, I believe. I'm sorry—"

"Don't apologize. We'd rather have you anyway." Owens was a grandfather and partial to young women. "I see we have Security as well as the two gentlemen who found the bones. And you, Dr. Ossum, must be here because it is your department that seems to be at the center of things. I take it that we don't have any reason yet to think that a theft has occurred?"

"We actually have more bones than we know what to do with. I don't quite know why such a fuss is being made about a few extra ones." Ulysses Ossum was Chairman of Anthropology, but he represented the digging archeologists. These archeologists, having the chairmanship, were currently the ascendant side of the department, much to the distress of the physical anthropologists, who saw little to be excited about in ancient bits of stone.

"There may be nothing to it at all, Dr. Ossum, but there seems to be a certain sentimental, if not scholarly, concern with the remains of Mr. Smithson. The Secretary feels that we should look into the matter so that we will not have to learn from the newspapers if anything is amiss."

"Something is clearly irregular. We don't like funny business almost as much as we don't like theft." Col. McKeown, Director of the Office of Protection Services, smiled as he said it, but that didn't mislead anybody. He never laughed about security.

"And we have Mr. Bader with us. Bobby, I want to see you after we adjourn—it's about getting me some decent curtains. But for now we'd better talk about your crypt."

Bobby Bader was the curator of the Smithsonian Castle and the Arts and Industries buildings. When the decision was made to restore these oldest of the Smithsonian Institution buildings, the restoration plans and selection of furnishings became the responsibility of newly hired Bobby Bader. The crypt, the sarcophagus and its contents were, accordingly, in his charge. "I should think that the first thing to do would be to return the bones to the sarcophagus. Then there should be a proximity alarm installed. Such a system has been in my budget for the past two submissions, but it has always been deleted." Bobby put the tips of his ten fingers together, and assumed his "I told you so" look. By nature, he stayed on the defensive. He was an architectural historian, but everybody, Owens included, treated him like an interior decorator.

"Is the top of the sarcophagus heavy? I think we should go look inside," suggested Henry.

"It is marble," said Bobby, "but it is not very large and the marble is cut thin. It should be easy enough to move."

"What could be in it?" demanded Col. McKeown. "A body? It is a bit small for a man, and besides, in this weather after a few days you wouldn't have to remove the top to know if a body were inside."

"Well," said Dr. Ossum, "our bones certainly don't stink, and I'm afraid I'm hardly concerned about the contents that do and are found in receptacles not under our jurisdiction."

"Nevertheless," persisted Henry, "it seems to me there must have been a reason why somebody would go to the trouble to remove and to hide the bones.

"A practical joke," suggested Miss Casey. "People are always playing practical jokes. You wouldn't believe what lawyers—"

"I don't believe it is a practical joke," said Hans, "because it was only an accident that I pulled out and measured the bones from that particular tray. A practical joke is only good if you can be sure upon whom it is played."

"—And can be certain that the victim is aware he has been victimized," Henry whispered to Hans.

Under Secretary Owens took charge of the meeting. "Mr. Scruggs, why do you think anything is in the sarcophagus? Col. McKeown's reasons why there couldn't be a body inside make sense to me."

"I just have a hunch, and I agree with Hans that the bones were too well hidden for it to be a joke."

"Well, then, let's see if you are right." Owens got to his feet and led the party downstairs to the crypt.

Henry stood back to allow the rest of the party to precede. He was naturally diffident. It also gave him a chance to size up Miss Casey. He knew she was an assistant general counsel and he had seen her from time to time in the Commons at lunchtime. Usually she had her nose buried in a book but he had not been able to tell what kind without getting close enough to look through the bottom part of his glasses. She wore glasses when she read. At least they had that in common. She also affected rather short skirts. Somehow that didn't go with the glasses. From his vantage point, now, three or four paces behind her, he could see that short skirts looked good on her. Unusual for ladies in their late twenties? Certainly unusual in lawyers.

The sarcophagus sat elevated on its plinth. It seemed serene and undisturbed, even elegant. Col. McKeown crossed the barrier and went close to the lid. He sniffed tentatively, then deeply. "Don't stink," he announced, and everyone relaxed. Col. McKeown turned on his radio phone and called for some guards to come and remove the lid. It proved to be relatively easy to pivot it in place so that the inside could be seen. Col. McKeown looked.

"Goddamn!" said the Colonel.

The Under Secretary jumped the barrier and moved in beside Col. McKeown. He looked down. "Goddamn!" he echoed.

There was a general scramble for the sarcophagus. Phoebe was too short to look in, so Henry picked her up. She felt nice. It was one of the few things about that day, when Henry looked back upon it, that he enjoyed.

The sarcophagus was not empty. In fact, it was so tightly packed that it was hard at first to tell exactly what was inside. Except that it seemed to be a body or at least pieces of one. The Colonel carefully plucked out one of the parts. It was a more or less complete leg. He weighed it in his hand.

"It is so light! It doesn't seem real!"

Ossum took it from him and examined it closely. "Freeze-dried," he announced. "At least I think so. We will have to ask somebody in Mammals to be sure."

Security took over and it was after six o'clock by the time the chamber had been photographed, checked for finger-prints, and the contents of the sarcophagus removed. The pieces of the body were assembled on the marble floor as

60

they emerged and the head was the last to be put in place. There was a gasp from the onlookers almost in unison. Miss Casey put it into words. "Bill of Rights!" She made it out into the entry hall before she lost her lunch.

It was indeed General Counsel William Wright. Col. McKeown laid out the pieces on the floor of the crypt. Henry checked and they all seemed to be there.

Henry climbed the sixty-two steps (thirty-one if you considered that they were two at a time) to his office and fetched a bottle of Scotch and one of sherry, the latter in deference to poor Miss Casey's upset stomach. The meeting reconvened in the Under Secretary's office.

"Miss Casey, perhaps you can tell us where Mr. Wright was supposed to be?"

"I'm not sure, Mr. Owens. He's been on vacation and I thought he intended to be back three weeks ago, but he was a little indefinite. He rented a cabin someplace in Maine. He had a lot of leave and there was a possibility he might be able to keep the cabin longer. Habeas—I mean, Mr. Bodde— may have heard from him."

"Well, the police can follow up things like that. I'm surprised we haven't heard from them already."

"Sir," said the Colonel, "Security has jurisdiction over anything that happens in the Castle. My detectives will take care of the investigation. I don't plan to call the police at this point in time." (Henry winced at "this point in time." He thought it must be left over from the colonel's days in the military.)

"How can you do that?" asked the Under Secretary. "The police have to be called in for a murder!"

"It's very complicated, sir. The Castle is not a part of the District of Columbia. We own and control the land outright."

"I believe he's right," said Miss Casey, who was recovering herself, "the Organic Act that set up the Smithsonian also set aside the land for the Castle. It's unique. The Castle is also outside the jurisdiction of the National Park Service."

"Miss Casey's got it exactly right, sir, the Park Service has it to the sidewalk in front of the Castle and the city picks it up at the sidewalk on Independence Avenue. Everything in between and west to the Freer Gallery and east to the A and I Building belongs to the Smithsonian."

"If that's so, why can't we set up a duty-free port, a casino?" Bobby Bader had intoxicating visions of turning his building into a profit-making enterprise. He also preferred thinking about anything at all except bodies in his crypt.

"A bawdy house," mused Henry aloud, combining the two.

"The Castle is still under U.S. jurisdiction. The FBI could still be involved for the violation of certain statutes," said Miss Casey firmly.

The Under Secretary was getting impatient. "I don't see how you can be sure Mr. Wright was killed in this building, whoever has jurisdiction over it. Does anybody know of a freeze-dry plant in the Castle?"

"Natural History," answered Hans. Henry poured him another drink.

"Exactly! He could have been killed in the Museum of Natural History. He certainly would have had to have been dried there."

"Or he might not have been murdered at all," observed McKeown. "A medical examiner will have to look at him."

"Colonel, I'm not a security specialist, but it seems to me that it must be rare for a man to commit suicide or die of natural causes and then to dismember himself and freeze the pieces. Call in the police. That's an order."

Even a colonel takes orders from the Under Secretary. Col. McKeown turned redder than usual and called the First District police. They all settled down to wait.

"I had thought it might be Kraft," said Henry when everybody else had become silent.

"Why? Why Kraft?" asked the Under Secretary.

"He should have been back on Monday. He isn't, and nobody's heard from him."

"He's in Ceylon shooting birds."

"We got a copy of a cable about Kraft from the American Embassy in Colombo to the Ceylon Desk at State. It said the Ceylonese cancelled his research permit. He apparently raved at the ambassador and left in a huff."

"He seems to like Paris and London a lot. Maybe he's consoling himself there." Owens did not like Kraft any more than anybody else did.

"Why do you suppose," asked Dr. Ossum, who was becoming interested in the matter despite his earlier pronouncement, "Mr. Wright was cut up like that?

"So he would fit in the sarcophagus, of course," said McKeown impatiently.

"No, I don't think so. If it had been only that, I believe the murderer would simply have found a larger container. There must have been a number of possibilities."

"The freeze-dry vacuum chamber," said Henry. "I've seen the one in the Natural History Building. I watched them do an albatross in it, but it isn't big enough for a whole human. You would have to take everything off the trunk and freeze them separately. You can't do it in a regular freezer because you need a vacuum to pull the moisture out. I don't know where you would find a bigger one."

Miss Casey was starting to turn pale again and Henry dropped the subject.

After a bit a police car pulled up in front of the Castle and in a couple of minutes a Smithsonian guard escorted two District policemen (one actually a policewoman) into the Under Secretary's office. McKeown went with them down to the crypt. The others stayed behind at the firm suggestion of the police. So it was that Henry did not witness the bawling out that McKeown received for moving the body and messing around with the crime scene. Word spread quickly through the guard force, however, and it was all reported to Henry the next day by Mr. Taggart. At last there was something to talk about besides the weather and the quantity of tourists on the Mall.

 **Six**

By the time Henry arrived at his office on Thursday morning (as usual, an hour late), there wasn't anybody at the Smithsonian who didn't know about the murder. (Only Col. McKeown still entertained the idea that it might not be murder.) Henry got on the phone right away and called up Olive.

"Is Dr. Kraft back from Ceylon yet?"

"Why?" demanded protective Olive.

"I have a number of foreign visitors who would like to see him," lied Henry.

"He's not available at the moment."

"When will he be?"

"I don't know," Olive admitted.

Henry was no sooner off the phone when the temporary secretary dropped a note on his desk:

MR. UNDER SECRETARY WANTS TO SEE YOU RIGHT NOW.

Henry hurried down the steps, as usual counting as he went. In an otherwise chaotic world, it was somehow reassuring that the number of steps always remained the same. He opened the door that led down the short flight of cast-iron steps into the tunnel. *56, 57, 58, 59, 60, 61, 62, 63. 63?* Damn, he must have miscounted. He had known when he started down the steps that he should have counted down from 62. Maybe he counted the top tread at the floor level in the tower. Did he usually count that one? He would be sure to check it when he got back.

The meeting had already started when he got to the Under Secretary's office. The same group as yesterday, but with the Director of the Natural History Museum, Dr. Carleton Parkes, and Mr. Dillyhay Plover, Director of Public Affairs, added, and Hans, unaccountably, missing. Working groups always got larger, never smaller. That was the rule. Once on one, you were never supposed to be dropped off just because the matter was not your concern.

"Mr. Bodde had to be in court this morning," Phoebe Casey was explaining. "He will try to attend future meetings."

"Come off it, Phoebe, Habeas Corpus never goes to meetings," said Mr. Plover, disagreeably, "he thinks it compromises his position if he gets involved in anything that might end up in court." Henry was no friend of Mr. Plover, but he felt he had a point there. Hayward Bode, known derisively as Habeas Corpus, was eccentric in the extreme and now that he was likely to be the Acting General Counsel there would be nobody to keep him in line. Henry took another look at Miss Casey. She would require some consoling.

"Please," said the Under Secretary, "let's get down to business. This morning's *Washington Post* only had a small article saying an unidentified body was found in the Castle. Even that story didn't make the edition I get at home. I haven't seen the early editions of the *Star* and the *Daily News* yet, but I presume they will have more information.

"Mr. Plover has been delaying returning calls from the press, but he'll have to talk to them some time this afternoon. We probably have an hour or so to get organized. I think we are agreed that dealing with the press should be left in the hands of the Office of Public Affairs."

"As long as we stick to the facts, what is the harm in any of us telling the press what we know?" asked Henry a bit naively. "Have we got anything to hide?"

"Mr. Scruggs," said Mr. Plover impatiently, "the Smithsonian has to be careful about its reputation. Something like this has to be explained to the press in just the right way. By a professional. That's why I am here."

"Oh."

"As a practical matter, everyone should refer all inquiries to Mr. Plover and he can forward to me any he feels he can't handle. You particularly, Mr. Scruggs, should not be placed in the position of speaking for the Smithsonian since you are, I believe, still employed by the Department of State." The Under Secretary's question was tinged with the barest hint of hostility. The Smithsonian was circling its wagons, and Henry was, after all, an Indian.

"What is it we are supposed to know, at this point?" asked Dr. Parkes. That was a stupid question, Henry thought. The answer was he wasn't supposed to know anything.

"Only that a body has been found in the Castle."

"Not any of the other details, Mr. Under Secretary?"

Mr. Plover handled that one. "There hasn't been a formal identification of the body and it only appears to have been cut up and freeze-dried. We don't admit to any of these details until they have been formally established. We also don't admit it was murder. There hasn't been an inquest yet. And because the press might try to get information from secondary sources, you had better not talk to your colleagues either."

"What about the location of the remains?" asked McKeown. He had been rather subdued since his dressing-down the previous evening, but was now considerably cheered that Mr. Dillyhay had joined him in denying it was murder.

"There will be no need to mention the crypt and certainly not the Smithson bones. They may have nothing to do with the case. As I said before, you people will say nothing to anybody and I will only say to the press, if asked, that a body has been found." Mr. Plover clearly had his position established. He would stonewall the affair and admit only those details already and conclusively revealed through other sources.

"Could I ask a question?" asked Henry.

"Please do so; your questions are always welcome." Perhaps the Under Secretary was showing his condescending side, or it could have been he was becoming irritated with Mr. Plover.

"Where is Dr. Kraft?"

"I don't see—" broke in Mr. Plover, but Under Secretary Owens shushed him.

"Quite so, Mr. Scruggs, Dr. Kraft is missing. Perhaps you could look for him."

"Yes, sir. I'll see if I can find out whether he has returned from abroad."

The Under Secretary looked around the room and evidently decided the meeting had gone on long enough. "Fine. You have your marching orders. I understand that the police will be calling on those of us who found the body, so keep yourselves available."

"Can't we just refer them to Mr. Plover?" asked Miss Casey. Nobody bothered to answer her, but Henry grinned at her and was rewarded by her warm hand under the conference table.

"Mr. Scruggs, will you stay on a minute? I have something else to talk to you about." The others filed out, some looking back, trying to decide whether Henry was going to be told something they should know about.

"Henry," said the Under Secretary, lapsing into the unfamiliar familiar, "do you know anything about the IPES?"

"Yes, sir, if you mean the International Publications Exchange Service. I have taken a number of foreign visitors out to look at it."

"Not much to look at, is it?"

"No, sir, but lots of foreign institutions depend on it for scientific journals and such, so visitors ask to see it. They are always disappointed."

"It used to be about the most important thing the Smithsonian did abroad. It goes way back."

"To about 1850, sir. I think it got its start sending American scholarly journals abroad on sailing ships."

"Well, there aren't any sailing ships anymore and there is a move to abolish it. It would save us about a half percent of our federal budget."

"Doesn't seem like very much."

"It isn't, if IPES is still actually doing some good. But it's a lot if it's a useless anachronism. I've been trying to find out which it is. I set up a committee almost a year ago to study the IPES. They don't seem to have come up with anything. Of course that's usual for committees. As you saw this morning, if anything gets done, it is usually due to one person."

"Mr. Plover?"

"I don't imagine you like him very much, but he has his uses. Fit right in at the State Department, I dare say. Anyway, when we found the remains of Mr. Wright yesterday it reminded me that I have to do something about IPES. Mr. Wright was the chairman of the IPES study group. I want you to take over."

"Me to succeed the General Counsel?" Henry paused in some confusion. There had to be a catch to it, but he couldn't immediately see what it was. "I'll of course do it if you want, but you surely know I would be resented. Everybody around here regards me as an outsider as it is. Who's on the committee?"

"The committee is made up of University Programs— that's Percy Jammers, of course; the Treasurer, Mr. Haley; Dr. Rebecca Haas—you may not know her—she is our Assistant Director of Libraries for Exchanges; and our missing Dr. Kraft."

"That's a rather high-level committee for me to head."

"That isn't what I had in mind. At this point I doubt if anybody could wake up the committee. I want you to do an independent study and report back directly to me."

"What about my boss?"

"Ambassador Craddock? I'll speak to him. He won't give you any trouble."

* * *

Henry called Miss Casey's office on the off chance that she might be willing to go to lunch. He had never actually spoken to her, let alone asked her out to lunch before. The receptionist in the Office of General Counsel asked Henry what his call was about. "Sex," he replied after a short pause. He almost said lunch but decided before he said it that if he had just wanted to have lunch, he could have asked Ronald Hipster or, God forbid, Dillyhay Plover.

Phoebe Casey came on the phone. She was laughing, so evidently the receptionist had told her the reason for the call. She would be delighted to have lunch, she said. What with the Under Secretary allowing Mr. Plover to put the clamp on discussions with her colleagues about the murder of the General Counsel, Miss Casey was going to burst if she couldn't talk to somebody.

"I think there are two murders," said Henry. They had a table in the Commons, where it was so crowded it was like talking confidentially on a rush-hour bus.

"Dr. Kraft?"

"Yes. Even the Under Secretary is worried. I could tell. As soon as I get back in the office I'm going to try to find out whether he came back to this country."

"Will the Immigration Service know?"

"Yes, but that would take forever. I'll get Travel to check with the airlines. There are only a few possibilities. It would be a direct flight, American carrier, probably from London and first class."

"First class?"

"Yes, he always travels first class because they won't let him ride up front with the pilot. It will be an American carrier because he is using up his federal travel funds. I have already looked at a copy of his travel orders. He had an open return."

"Who do you think killed Mr. Wright?" Phoebe was not really very much interested in Dr. Kraft.

"I think it was the same person who killed Kraft."

"If he is dead."

"Exactly. But I think he is. I just don't know why and how."

"Or who, or maybe when," added practical Phoebe. "Mr. Wright's body must have made at least one trip over the Mall. Do you suppose the murderer got a property pass to get him out of the Natural History Building?" She rounded her eyes in horror at the thought.

"We could check the passes. The guards keep them on file forever. I've noticed they never really read them."

She smiled rather sickly. "We might prepare a property pass: arms (two), legs (two), trunk (one), and head (one), freeze-dried remains, property of the General Counsel's estate. We could make up boxes and see if the guards would let them be taken out without looking inside."

"Actually, I think it was the tunnel."

"What tunnel?"

"The one for the steam pipes that crosses the Mall between the Castle and the Natural History Building. I'm told the guards have occasionally used it when there have been things like riots."

"The murderer would still have to get around inside the buildings."

"I've been thinking about that. It would be difficult but not impossible. The Natural History Museum is full of cabinets on wheels. On a summer weekend evening you could roll one all over the place without being challenged, particularly in the basement staff areas. Once you got the body into the tunnel, it would be simple to bring it over to the Castle. The tunnel leads to the middle of the east-west corridor in the basement of the Castle. A few feet west from that point there is a door into the stairs by the public toilet. If you pick your time right to avoid the janitors, you would never meet anybody there after hours. The stairs lead up to the first-floor main entry hall within just a few feet of the crypt. Since the main door is always shut after the building closes to the public, that is a dead-end area and the guards almost never patrol it."

"But there are glass doors leading out onto the front

steps. Tourists are always pressing their noses against the glass after hours. You can see their nose-prints in the morning. They could have seen the murder!" Phoebe's eyes opened with horror as if seeing through the front door of the Castle pieces of a body being carried hither and yon.

"I suppose you don't get involved in murders like this unless you enjoy taking chances." Henry's mind was wandering from the murder. He decided Phoebe was charming. True, she was a lawyer and that was a count against her, but she might have been an auditor or something like that, so perhaps lawyer wasn't so bad.

After lunch, Henry climbed up to his office. He counted the steps again. Sixty-two counting the top step. He must have miscounted this morning.

Henry picked up the phone to dial Travel and caught an incoming call from IIE before it rang.

"*Hello? Mr. Scruggs?*"

Damn! "Yes?"

"*This is Tomlinson, over at IIE. Say, that Dr. Sabuki told me about something funny that happened over at your place last week. Were those really Smithson's bones you found?*"

"It's possible. Could also be computer failure." Henry thought that always sounded plausible.

"*Well, anyway, I've got another visitor for you. Dr. Kunjeer. She's a historian of technology. Wants to see your Air and Space Museum.*"

"I'd like to see it, too. We're just getting ready to build it. We've been getting ready to build it since the end of World War II."

"*You've got something over there with airplanes in it. I took my son to see it.*"

"Yeah, we've got some exhibits in the Arts and Industries Building, and there's an old hangar out back with some stuff. Mostly models."

"*What's the holdup on the museum?*"

"Congress has insisted we wait until the war was over. First Korea and now Vietnam. A ceiling was placed on the cost of the museum years ago so the size of the museum changes inversely with inflation. It started out as big as all outdoors, but if we don't hurry up and build it, it will eventually be about the size of a birdhouse."

"Okay, well, show her what you've got. But she's got to see it tomorrow morning. That's the only time she's got free."

"I can't get a docent and certainly not a curator on such short notice."

"Can't you take her through? She's a looker."

Henry reluctantly agreed to do it. He would just have to put off starting on IPES. And the Indian woman might indeed be a looker, though probably Tomlinson just said that to keep Henry from turning him down.

Henry hurriedly dialed Travel before anybody else could call him. He wanted a cup of tea desperately but it would have to wait. Travel grumbled and Henry had to make dark hints before they would do it, but they finally said they would search for Kraft's trail.

Teatime in the Foreign Affairs Office was generally the high point of the day. It could run from three until five if there was anything interesting to talk about, and today there was. Other offices have endless and unproductive staff meetings, usually in the mornings. FAO spurned such in favor of the more genteel teatime. It had been Henry's idea, but it was well received by everyone who counted in FAO. Small matters of business were discussed and quickly dispensed with, and then the conversation could move on to more interesting things, usually gossip.

In spite of his dignity, Ambassador Craddock liked gossip and often joined the staff at teatime, but today he was absent, being over at State at a retirement party for a former colleague. Today his deputy, Ronald Hipster, was nominally in charge. Ronald was a former instructor in international relations at the Emmetstown (North Dakota) Community College and was, in Henry's opinion, certifiable, and likely had been given to the Smithsonian on a work-release program from St. Elizabeth's. He always took tea.

The third member of the office, Gerald Blackman, was the

only experienced foreign affairs specialist in the office, unless one counted Henry. It was Blackman who did all the work and consequently he felt much overworked and put-upon. He joined in tea when there was business to discuss and usually retired with his cup to his desk as soon as the group moved on to pleasanter things. But not today.

Dreamy Weekes was also a regular. Some claimed that Dreamy had been known to come in for tea on her vacation when particularly good gossip was afoot. When sessions were otherwise dull, she used the time to tease the boys, especially Ronald, because he blushed helplessly, and even on occasion could be made to stammer. Dreamy took sugar in her tea, even in oolong, so Henry didn't trust her even though he lusted after her.

"Henry, Sweetie," said Dreamy, "we are waiting to hear what happened last night. The Smithsonian is alive with rumors."

"I'm sure I don't know. I got in late this morning."

"You always get in late, so that's no excuse." Blackman disapproved of Henry's habitual late work hours. He came in early every day and left promptly at five-fifteen to catch his car pool.

"I've checked on you, Henry. You had a meeting with Mr. Owens late yesterday and you never came back. I stayed here waiting for you till late." Dreamy stuck out her bosom and swung one leg over the other, showing a considerable portion of thigh. She did things like that when she was lying or teasing, which to her were one and the same.

Hipster, whose attention had been wandering but had returned home at the sight of Dreamy's semiprivate parts, spoke up. "Henry, old man, it is your duty to keep us informed. Fess-up!" Hipster's words were slurred and Henry realized he was drunk again. Ronald often had cocktails in a topless bar for lunch.

"I am sorry, but I am under orders not to tell you that Bill of Rights's dismembered remains, freeze-dried, were found in Smithson's tomb."

"Who found them?" demanded Blackman.

"What about the Constitution?" asked Hipster, who was having a hard time following the conversation.

"I can't tell you that I told them to look."

"Did it have anything to do with the Smithson remains you found last week?" Blackman had learned about that discovery at a previous teatime.

"I am not allowed to say."

"And who was this Mr. Under who called you to a meeting just before lunch?" Dreamy demanded to know.

"Where did you hear that?"

"Little Miss Temposec told me."

"She got it wrong. I was called to a meeting with my undercover agent." The phone rang. It was Travel. Kraft had returned on Pan American on August 7th. "I bet he's dead, too," said Henry after he hung up. His colleagues looked at him curiously. "They haven't silenced me on Kraft yet."

On the last Friday in August, Henry was late again as usual. He had a better excuse than usual, however, because his *Washington Post* had arrived late and he had lingered to read the article about the murder at the Smithsonian. The paper had learned surprisingly little, only that the body of a murdered man had been found in the Castle and that it was thought to be General Counsel William Wright. The scent of unrequited curiosity ran through the article and several officials including the Secretary had been quoted as saying "no comment."

Sixty-two steps (by actual count) and Henry panted at the top of the stairs. A new temporary secretary greeted him. "Did you wish to see someone, sir?" She was pretty, this one, but Henry noticed a wedding ring right off.

"No, I don't want to see anybody; I just want to sit down." He stumbled into his office and sat heavily in his chair.

The new girl looked at him with dismay but when he started going through the morning mail, she decided he might belong there. "Are you Mr. Scruggs?"

"I'm from the IRS. We may want you to testify if we get the goods on him."

She grinned. Quicker than average, Henry thought. "The *Washington Post* has called twice. A Mr. Harrison wants you to call him back."

"Thanks," said Henry as he dropped the call slip into the wastebasket. "I'll pay the paperboy directly." He looked at his watch. He would have to hustle to meet Dr. Kunjeer downstairs by ten o'clock.

Dr. Mira Kunjeer was, to Henry's surprise, quite attractive. Hardly the looker promised by Tomlinson, but no slouch. She wore her sari in such a way that he could not tell whether she had anything on underneath it. His sidelong looks as he tried to find out seemed to amuse her. She was quite Western in some respects with a Midwestern American accent. She had attended the University of Michigan, she admitted.

Henry showed her the usual things: the *Apollo 11* command module, the backup lunar lander, *Friendship 7,* working back into conventional flight with the supersonic *Bell X-1* and the *Spirit of St. Louis,* and onto the early experiments with the Wright Flyer and the model of the Langley Aerodrome.

The East Range held a new ballooning exhibit that was attractive and doubtless of much historical importance but short on technology, Dr. Kunjeer's real interest. The new World War I exhibit just about to open in the West Range of the A&I was still closed off and inaccessible. The fuselage of what appeared to be a Fokker D-7 was being moved into the area, but little else could be viewed of the new exhibition.

There wasn't much else to see in the A&I Building, so they visited the old exhibits out in the World War I vintage aircraft hangar out back, next to Independence Avenue. As they left the hangar and walked in the disappearing shade along the west wall of the A&I Building, they passed several huge experimental rockets. High up on the side of one was a liquid oxygen port labeled LOX. It was always good for a laugh and Henry pointed out that the lack of a port for BAGELS had doomed the rocket from the first.

That reminded them that they were hungry and Henry invited Dr. Kunjeer to lunch in the Smithsonian Commons. The late August heat was uncomfortable ("It feels like Calcutta," Dr. Kunjeer said), so they walked toward the close by south door in the basement of the Castle.

Dr. Kunjeer wrinkled up her nose. "It smells like Calcutta, too."

"That's the beetle factory." Henry pointed to a small two-story building between the hangar and the Freer Gallery, just south of the Castle. "We keep dermestid beetles there. They are used to eat the flesh off of the carcasses of animals for the Museum of Natural History collections. The beetles don't damage the bone."

"Ugh!" said Dr. Kunjeer with feeling.

It didn't bother her appetite, however, and they both had hearty lunches from the Commons buffet. She admired the gothique groin-work of the room and averted her eyes from the horrid carpeting. They talked about airplanes and Henry described the aircraft collections out at the Smithsonian's Silver Hill storage facility. Dr. Kunjeer regretted that she didn't have enough time to go out to see them. She was taking the 5 P.M. shuttle to New York.

"Mr. Scruggs," she said over tea, "in classical times Indian women didn't wear tops."

"I've heard that."

"I thought you might like to know."

Henry saw Dr. Kunjeer to the door and returned to his office. Sixty-two steps and holding, he observed with satisfaction. He had counted with only half his mind. The other half was chewing away on murder problem. He sat at his desk and looked at the mess on top. The profile of overseas research was now long neglected. He could go out to the IPES offices in Anacostia and begin his survey, but it was much more fun to follow the scent of murder. Scent! It was the thought of the scent that did it. He picked up the phone and called Hans.

"Hans, would you like to find another body?"

"Sure, why the hell not."

"I think I may know where Dr. Kraft is."

"In the Natural History Museum?"

"In Anthropology."

"We don't have any freeze-dried bodies."

"He hasn't been freeze-dried.

"Then he would surely stink," said Hans with certainty.

"Not if he didn't have any flesh left."

"How would they do that?"

"They would use the beetle factory to eat him up."

"God in heaven!"

"You think it's possible?"

"It could be, but how do we find him? We have an awful lot of skulls, you know. Over fifteen thousand at last count."

"There's always dentistry. I don't suppose your usual specimens have modern fillings."

"No, but it would be a lot of work to look at every skull that closely. It would take a lot of people a long time." Hans paused to make some calculations. *"About half a man-year if you had to handle each one."*

"Wouldn't there be other differences, ones easier to spot at just a glance?

"Well, there would be mineral deposits. Bone is porous and after it's been buried it picks up minerals. The color changes. And dust. New specimens aren't dusty."

"I don't suppose our murderer would go so far as to fake things like that?"

"The only way to find out is to look. I'll call you back."

The calendar was off just enough for the weekend to miss by one day being the Labor Day long weekend. Still, Henry remembered from the previous week how long two days could be. He called Phoebe before she left her office to arrange a date, but she was (so she said) otherwise engaged. Henry tried Dreamy at the last moment but she claimed she had to do something with her husband. She also said she didn't date honkies but then she crossed her legs which probably meant that was a lie. For a moment Henry thought about trying to catch Dr. Kunjeer and ask her to delay her

77

trip to New York, but it was late and she would already have left for the airport. Too bad, he would have liked to have unwrapped her sari.

As Henry went home alone on Friday evening, he felt that at forty-two he was over the hill. He was beginning to take seriously the State Department career development officer who had told him that he was too "long in the tooth" for the political officer assignment he had wanted the year before, one that would have advanced his career in the Foreign Service. They had wanted to ship him off to Australia for five years in a different assignment that would have done nothing but make him five years older. When it was over and he returned, he would have been so long in the tooth he wouldn't have been able to get his mouth shut.

But Henry had had a friend in Personnel who had given him a chance to redirect his career. A detail as a liaison officer at the Smithsonian might let him find something for which he was better suited. But thus far he hadn't had notable success.

Friday night it rained and cooled down enough so he could keep on his shoes and could play his piano. He worked on the big Clementi G major sonata, but came to realize that he had to find a new piano tuner. Clementi, who was after all one of the great London piano builders, was not happy with an out-of-tune instrument. Henry's last tuner must have been a Mayan Indian. Henry didn't care to try tuning it himself. A harpsichord with only one string per note is one thing, but a piano with as many as three strings and those under vastly greater tension, was something else. He would call the Division of Musical Instruments at the Museum of History and Technology on Monday morning and get them to suggest someone. He was glad now that Monday wasn't a holiday.

Saturday he spent the day wandering around the National Gallery and trying to strike up conversations with apparently unattached females. He finally cornered one who was looking perplexedly at an El Greco. She was at least sixty-five and from Omaha, but she was sociable enough and Henry was getting along with her just fine until her daughter showed up and glared at Henry for trying to take advantage of an old lady probably for her money. Funny, she hadn't looked rich.

Henry fled from the National Gallery and drove out to Bethesda before Dale Music closed and bought a new Wiener Ur-Text edition of the Haydn sonatas. He played through them on Saturday evening, tuning be damned, then went to bed with a glass of Scotch, a can of salted almonds, and Samuel Cole Williams's *History of the Lost State of Franklin.*

His sleep was untimely disturbed at eleven-thirty on Sunday morning by a call from Hans.

"I didn't wake you, did I?"

"Of course you did. It's the middle of the morning."

"I thought you would want to know I found them!"

Henry was silent. He was actually fishing for his glasses on his bedside table.

"Are you there? I found the bones! Clean as a—what you call it—a thistle."

"That's whistle. That's what we Americans say when something is really clean. I don't know why. Where are you now?"

"I'm in my laboratory. Are you coming down?"

"As soon as I can get dressed and fix some tea. Wait for me."

"Okay, but hurry. It's almost lunchtime."

"Hans? Don't hang up!"

"Yeah?"

"Better lock your office door."

 **Seven**

The murderer had knocked out a number of the teeth, but he had missed a front tooth with a porcelain filling. It was a dead giveaway, so to speak.

"You see how white and even the coloring is on the skull. This was living bone until very recently." Hans held up the mystery skull alongside an obviously old one.

Henry looked at the new one, not wanting to touch it. It bore an accessions number. He wrote it down. "Can we check this number out?

Hans turned on his computer and began the search. Surprisingly enough, the number was already in the computer accessions file. It was for a specimen already on file, a giant sloth, estimated at sixty thousand years old. "No, I don't think so," he said looking again at the skull.

"I think our murderer has a sense of humor. Hans, have you got a Smithsonian phone book? I think we ought to call the Under Secretary and Security."

Under Secretary Owens proved to be easier to convince than did McKeown. McKeown couldn't at first see anything sinister in a clean human skull with a porcelain filling that claimed to be an ancient sloth. But in a little while, his investigators had arrived and taken over. Henry and Hans were chased away. They went to get a late lunch, but anyplace you'd want to eat was already closed. On inspiration, Henry suggested Wilkerson's Restaurant near Potomac Beach. It was a long drive and they were starving when they got there, but they had a fine early supper.

First thing Monday morning (Henry's first thing; everybody else's late morning), Henry went over to the Smithsonian library to see Rebecca Haas, Assistant Director for Exchanges. It had either been to do that or be almost certain to be called out of his office for another meeting with Dillyhay Plover about the second body. Henry simply wasn't prepared for that.

The Smithsonian Institution Libraries (SIL), as might be expected in a major research institution, is a large and complex operation. Its principal offices occupy much of the ground floor, north side, of the Natural History Museum. Most of the bureaus (museums, research facilities, etc.) of the Institution have their own branch libraries, as do even many of the curatorial departments, such as the Department of Anthropology, and these branches are scattered throughout the Smithsonian. In a sense, the Smithsonian library system is similar to a city library system with branches all around town.

Henry was intimidated from the start. Dr. Haas was six feet tall in flat shoes, which she spurned in favor of high heels. Willowy, sturdy, and forty came to Henry's mind when she looked down at him.

"You said something about IPES? What do you want to know about it?"

"I just wanted to let you know that the Under Secretary has asked me to take a look at it."

"Whatever for? There's already a committee doing that! I'm a member of it. Can he have forgotten?" Dr. Haas blanched, then looked terrifyingly irritated.

"I don't know what's on his mind. He just told me to do it, so I have to, but I thought I ought to let you know. He told me about the committee."

"Do you have some sort of qualifications in this field?"

"No, none at all. Maybe that's the reason. Maybe he wanted an unbiased viewpoint."

"I think you had better keep away from IPES. I'll just have a talk with Mr. Owens. Now, is there anything else you wanted? I'm busy." She was composed again, even icy.

Henry did not time the interview, but if he had, he would have found it was under five minutes. He had taken up very little of her time. Ignoring her orders, he proceeded directly from the Natural History Museum and out to Anacostia to the warehouse that housed the IPES.

IPES got its start in the mid-nineteenth century at a time of revolution when many countries were nervous about the flow of publications into their borders. It was also a time when the United States was emerging as a major contributor to world literature in science, technology, and other scholarship.

Joseph Henry, the founding Secretary, in the first years conceived a role for the Smithsonian to facilitate the flow of these publications between the United States and other nations. This involved the gathering together of publications from many U.S. institutions, sending them abroad, arranging for them to pass unhindered across foreign boundaries, and having them distributed to individual foreign institutions by various central libraries, scientific societies, and the like. Similarly, the Smithsonian received shipments of publications from foreign sources and distributed them throughout the United States.

IPES was one of a number of Joseph Henry's inspired creations. These derived from his central idea of establishing a global network of scholars in research and publication. Thus he proposed the use of the evolving telegraph network to chart the dynamics of weather systems as they moved across North America. This pioneering Smithsonian program eventually grew and was spun off as the National Weather Bureau. Dr. Henry's idea for an international service of observatories reporting transient cosmic phenomena eventually grew into the Smithsonian Astrophysical Observatory. His ideas about the Smithsonian charting the earth's magnetic fields unfortunately did not take root as a lasting program, though the name "Henry" was given to the basic unit of inductance in this field.

So important did IPES become by the end of the nineteenth century, that the Smithsonian was given responsibility, under treaty, for the exchange of official government documents in addition to its traditional scholarly exchanges. By the turn of the century, IPES had more than twenty employees, a huge operation considering the size of the Smithsonian at the time.

Following World War II, the increased ease with which American and foreign librarians could exchange documents caused the flow of traffic through IPES to diminish steadily. Nevertheless, a hard core of business continued through the third quarter of the century despite efforts to cut down on the flow. Many foreign countries continued to use IPES, as did a surprising number of U.S. universities, medical centers, and scientific societies.

As IPES staff members died or otherwise retired, the Smithsonian scavenged jobs, slots as they were called, from the withering organization. By the time Henry arrived to study it, there were only three people left: a senior mail clerk on temporary assignment to IPES, a laborer, and a college student working part time.

What Henry saw during his first morning shocked him. Because of the continuing volume of publications and the chronic understaffing, IPES had become little more than a postal subsidy, with overseas or domestic postage being stamped on the packages, according to the direction of the flow. Foreign countries were still shipping things to IPES by ocean freight, for distribution within the United States by the Smithsonian. But for the most part, packages coming from institutions in the United States were going abroad by air showing the Smithsonian as sender. Gone were the days when IPES developed sources of publications at home and abroad. The occasional new customer learned of IPES by word of mouth.

Henry had intended to stay at IPES for the whole day, digging into the old files (new files were sketchy since the present staff had little time to generate paperwork) and working up statistics, but a call came through for him from Hans.

"Henry? Your office said you might be over there. You hiding out from the press? They've been after me all morning. What should I do?"

"They told us at the last meeting not to talk to them, but you weren't there. Did anybody call you and tell you not to talk to the press?"

"Nobody told me anything."

"In your place I would try to get the press to pay me for a story. Have you found out anything about your porcelain filling?"

"That's why I called. Kraft doesn't have any."

"Fillings?"

"Teeth!"

Henry decided he'd better get back to the Castle for a skull session, even if it meant another go-around with Plover. He was sure the Under Secretary would be calling a meeting. As it was, he arrived in time to eat at the Commons before the buffet was down to light bread and cold cuts. Hamilton Sealyham and Taylor Maidstone were at a corner table with their heads together.

"May I join you?"

"Please do, Mr. Ambassador." Hamilton scrambled to clear a place for Henry's tray. "Taylor and I were just discussing the grisly happenings in our family keep."

"Rumor has it," said Taylor who was ever direct, "that it was you who found Bill of Rights. Was it because you had some reason to have inside information on where to look? You can tell me; I won't tell anybody." That was Taylor's way of announcing that he would tell everybody he met. It was also his way of suggesting that Henry might have murdered the General Counsel, a thought which, oddly enough, had not before occurred to Henry.

"Actually, I have dismissed the first murder from my mind, and now I'm on to the next."

"Wha—what? Tell me, is there really another one?" Hamilton tipped over his glass of wine with excitement.

"I'm not sure. First I need to know who's missing."

"Practically everybody," said Taylor. "Hardly anybody gets back until after Labor Day. I wouldn't be here myself if they hadn't taken away my travel money. Of course I might have stayed around anyway if I could have been sure of being on hand at the departure of certain persons in this institution."

"Mr. Kraft is still missing, I believe. Taylor, here, tried to see him this morning and Olive was more opaque than usual."

"Opaque? How can you be more opaque than usual? Opaque is opaque. I just said her eyes looked like those of a week-old fish."

"Surely you mean a week-dead fish. But it isn't Kraft," said Henry to break up this rather peripheral argument.

"It isn't Kraft?! Then there is another body! Oh my! Oh my! Out with it!" demanded Hamilton. Hamilton didn't actually bounce on his chair, but he came close to it and the chair's joints grunched.

Henry explained about the dermestid beetles and his hunch, and the finding of the skull that wasn't a sloth, but which had teeth so it wasn't Kraft either. "So now we have to find out just who it is."

"Certainly that is one question, but one might also ask who is the murderer?" Taylor bestowed a gargoylish grin on his companions.

"I certainly don't have inside knowledge," said Hamilton. "Far from it, in fact. But approaching it purely from the point of view of likely candidates for murder, I do think you might wish to be in touch with Percy Jammers's dentist."

Henry was right. When he made it back to his office (63 steps again; he was counting an extra one somewhere or perhaps he was counting the two paces on the landing), there was a message waiting for him to come back over to the Castle for a meeting with the Under Secretary. He noticed that the hand that gave him the message no longer had a wedding ring on it. Had she become divorced over the weekend? Had she lost it down the drain whilst doing the dishes? He would look into it if he ever had the time. And if she were still there when he got back. Then, again, there was Phoebe and maybe he wouldn't bother.

It was a small meeting this time: Hans, McKeown, Plover, and Phoebe. That surprised Henry since he expected the unofficial Smithsonian Murders Working Group to grow with each new event.

The Under Secretary called the meeting to order. "We have a preliminary autopsy on the General Counsel. It appears that his skull was fractured. The coroner has never worked on a freeze-dried body before so he is reluctant to say that the fracture was the cause of death. However, no other, more probable, cause has been discovered."

"Had it been anybody else, decapitation might have been a contributing cause." It was a surprising remark from Miss Casey, but, then, she had never been too fond of Mr. Wright.

The Under Secretary chose not to hear her. "Mr. Scruggs, you know that the skull of the second body is not that of Mr. Kraft. Does your intuition suggest whose it might be?"

"Yes, of course. I think Mr. Percy Jammers was the last owner."

Mr. Plover waded in: "We can't afford to have irresponsible speculation, Mr. Under Secretary. It is all I can do to manage the facts that are known."

"Which are not any," put in Miss Casey sarcastically.

"Exactly. We don't know anything so we mustn't speculate." Mr. Plover did not often recognize sarcasm when he encountered it, which was odd because it was so often.

"This is not speculation," Henry said recklessly. "I have a confidential source of information."

"You can't withhold information like that! You could be prosecuted for impeding an investigation." McKeown gave Henry his most intimidating stare.

"Okay, I got it in the confessional."

"But you're not a priest! What were you doing in a confessional?"

"I just said that to mislead you because you won't believe the truth."

"Scruggs, quit wasting my time!" The Under Secretary was losing patience.

"Yes, sir! I got the information from tarot cards."

"That's idiotic," said Mr. Plover.

"See! I told you nobody would believe me!"

"This meeting is adjourned." People got up to leave and the Under Secretary spoke to Henry. "Stay a few moments, Scruggs, I want to talk to you."

When the room was cleared and the door was closed, Mr. Owens sat there just looking at Henry. Henry broke the silence. "Sir, the suggestion about Jammers comes from the two biggest gossips in the Institution. I don't know that they're right, but Jammers is missing and, once again, it feels right."

"I thought it might be something like that. The other possibility is that you are a double murderer. I'll have it checked."

"Which, sir?" asked Henry uncomfortably.

"Both, probably. In the meantime I received a call from Dr. Haas. She was very upset. I'm not quite sure why you felt you had to tell her what you were up to. What did you say to her?"

"I said very little; she didn't give me much chance. She ordered me not to study IPES. I only told her because it was likely she would find out anyway. I thought she ought to hear it from me."

"You didn't go to any of the other members of the IPES committee?"

"No. One is dead, and two are missing. That only leaves Dr. Haas and the Treasurer. It seemed to me that she was the only one directly involved with IPES. She must send publications through IPES all the time."

"Yeah, I suppose that makes sense. What do you think of her order for you to keep out of it?"

"I'm ignoring it for the moment. I was out in Anacostia this morning. If Dr. Haas succeeds you as Under Secretary, I'll reevaluate the situation."

It ought to be cooler today, it now being September, Henry thought as he climbed the steps. Sixty-two again, maybe this was going to be a good day. The new temporary secretary was still there. He leaned on the post at the top of the steps and panted. "Any messages?"

"Yes, sir, you should call Mrs. Saldana at IIE."

"God! Not another one!"

"I'm sorry, sir."

"It isn't your fault, it is just that the place is overrun with foreign visitors this summer. They should go somewhere where it is nice and cool." It was no use. She still was without the ring, but how can you ask anybody for a date when they call you "sir"? Henry dragged himself into his office, collapsed in his chair, picked up his phone, and dialed IIE.

"Yes, this is Mrs. Saldana."

"This is Henry Scruggs at the Smithsonian. I believe you called?"

Mrs. Saldana wanted to send over a Costa Mangoan lady, Mrs. Ferro y Silva, who wanted to know all about museums. When? First thing tomorrow morning, of course.

When Henry got off the phone he was late for tea and the others were already started. The Fig Newtons were gone, but there were some slightly stale ginger cookies. Henry regaled the others with the latest developments, fact and gossip. Even Ambassador Craddock was entertained, and sat attentively, playing with his small white mustache until he realized it was after five-fifteen and he was on his own time.

In the morning, Mrs. Ferro y Silva was waiting for Henry when he arrived. Someone had put a cup of coffee in her hand, but she was clearly impatient. Henry said he was sorry to have kept her waiting, but she ignored his apology.

Mrs. Saldana had not prepared him for Mrs. Ferro. "My good friend, the Minister of Education, he has appointed me to head a study commission on museums. I come to the Smithsonian to learn everything!" She gave Henry a reflexive golden smile. Insincere, but lined with the treasury of Costa Mango.

"How long do you have in Washington?" Henry expected the usual three hours before plane time.

"Six months, but I can extend it if I wish." Henry sat in stunned silence as she went on: "First you must tell me where I can live!"

"Where are you staying now?"

"I just arrive this morning."

"But Mrs. Saldana arranged your appointment yesterday."

"Yes, I call her from Miami. I come straight here. The suitcases, they are with the guard downstairs. They are okay there, no?" When she got no argument, Mrs. Ferro proceeded to other things. She gave Henry an appraising look and appeared to make up her mind. "Maybe I can stay in your house?"

Henry spent the rest of the morning trying to find someplace, other than his office, for Mrs. Ferro to do her internship. Ordinarily, the best possibility was the Office of Museum Training, but everybody there was gone until after Labor Day. Similarly, the hotels were full until after the holiday and there was no place to lodge her.

At lunchtime, Mrs. Ferro announced she was hungry and wished to be fed. Henry gave up any hope of getting work done and took her over to the Commons to eat. He found Phoebe there, sitting by herself at a table for two. Damn Mrs. Ferro y Whatever!

After lunch, Henry sat Mrs. Ferro down at the office conference table with every book he could find on the Smithsonian—annual reports, handouts, enough to keep her busy for a week, or until the training office got back into business. In mid-afternoon, the call came for what had become the daily meeting of the Murder Working Group. Henry hurried down the steps with so much on his mind that he forgot to count steps until he had descended to the second floor. Damn!

"Once again," said Under Secretary Owens, "Mr. Scruggs has found us a murder. The remains we discussed yesterday are those of Mr. Jammers."

The office filled with excited chatter until the Under Secretary held up his hand to quieten the group. "The police wish to speak to Mr. Scruggs, probably tomorrow."

"You can't tell them anything," said Mr. Plover. "We can't be sure they won't talk to the press."

"Mr. Scruggs doesn't have a choice in the matter," said McKeown in a rare burst of practicality tinged with regret, "and neither do we."

"For your information," continued the Under Secretary, "we can find no cause of death for Mr. Jammers. Because of the condition of the remains, the coroner felt that a forensic anthropologist could do a better job determining the cause of death. Consequently, we have had Dr. Mayes look at the skeleton. He has found no abnormalities. I fear the dermestid beetles have eaten any other evidence.

"This is discouraging, because I have a growing feeling that we have not reached the end of these unfortunate occurrences. Mr. Kraft still seems to be missing and there may be others. People around this place are so casual about coming into the office that you can't be sure."

Phoebe held up her hand. How pretty it is, thought Henry.

"Yes, Miss Casey? You don't have to be recognized, just break right in. Everybody else does."

"Mr. Owens, sir, I have an idea about finding Mr. Kraft."

"What is that?"

"It is obvious that the murderer is being clever about putting bodies in places where bodies will not seem out of place. What we should do is think about the other places in the Smithsonian where we keep bodies."

"This is silly," said Mr. Plover. "There aren't any."

"We certainly have dummies in the dioramas in Natural History," said Dr. Ossum, "and the National Collection of Fine Art has statues. I hope we aren't expected to break them all up looking for a body inside."

"Not unless they are new ones," said Phoebe. "But I don't think our murderer would just dip the body in plaster or bronze it. That has already been done in fiction, and he is more original than that."

"How do you know?" asked McKeown.

"Know what? That the murderer is original?"

"No, that the murderer is a he. It might be a woman."

Phoebe thought about that one. "I suppose it might. But I doubt it."

"Mummies," said Henry, almost to himself.

"I am not a mother! And I don't see what that's got to do with it."

"He's right," said Dr. Ossum with surprise. "The murderer could wrap up the victim and file it with our mummy collection. We've got lots and nobody's notice it."

"They would after a few days." McKeown was still hot on the scent.

"I'll bet," said Phoebe, "that the murderer mummified the body. He—or she—wouldn't do anything less than a proper job of it."

The Under Secretary sighed. "We'll have to X-ray the entire lot of them, I suppose."

"Remember, Kraft's dental records showed he had false teeth," Hans reminded them. "If they are left in, they will be easy to find, but if the murderer pocketed them, you won't be able to identify the body."

"Not quite so," Ossum corrected him. "Egyptian mummies generally had at least some of their teeth. If we find one without any, it will be suspicious and we will have to analyze the windings."

The meeting broke up with everybody, even Mr. Plover, eager for the hunt. Dr. Ossum would set his Anthropology Department to work right away, examining the mummies.

Henry walked with Phoebe as far as the stairs to her office, two floors above. "I wanted to see you at lunch, but your table was too small. I was stuck with a woman from Costa Mango."

"I should have thought you would have been happy to have her all to yourself. She is quite abundant in those features men seem to like."

"She is the mistress of the Minister of Education. I assume he gave her a grant to get rid of her for a while. But the hotels are full and she doesn't have a place to stay. Can you put her up?"

"Don't try to push her off on me! I should think that if you have a double bed, she would be happy enough. She would crowd a single." Phoebe turned and started climbing the stairs. Her behind wiggled seductively. Henry wondered how many steps there were to her floor.

 **Eight**

Henry was uncharacteristically secretive about the next few days, including the long Labor Day weekend. He did, in fact, put those days totally out of his own mind. Later, when it became possible to think about it, he justified himself by saying, to himself, that he had been rather put out with Phoebe at the time. Not, of course, that he had to answer to Phoebe for anything. For the moment, at least, he was determined to put Mrs. Ferro y Silva right out of his mind.

Coming at the end of the silly season, the Smithsonian murders, two of them at least, got a big play in the papers over the long weekend. Henry, who had been otherwise engaged, had not bothered to read about them.

Be that as it may, Henry arrived (*57, 58, 59, 60, 61,* Ah ha! *62,* all is right with the world!) at his office after the holiday with renewed determination to find somewhere else for Mrs. Ferro y Silva to sleep, if she ever found it necessary to do so.

By noon, Henry had made arrangements for her to stay at the International Student House and for her training to be supervised by the Office of Museum Training. The price of the latter was having to listen on the telephone while the OMT director fussed about all the times other offices, including Foreign Affairs, had tried to cut themselves in on the training of foreigners, a function that was ordained in the Creation rightfully to belong to OMT. Henry scrooched up his shoulder to hold the telephone and got back to searching country files for data to put in his overseas research survey. He was through with Haiti (studies of voodoo rituals related to solar eclipses, bioenergetics of coral reefs, and the niche ecology of grasshoppers), Honduras (microlepidoptera, canopy beetles, lichens, and mating behavior of birds of paradise), and was well into Hungary (medieval jewelry, nineteenth-century itinerant artists, polymorphism in hymenoptera, and nest-building by graniverous birds, thus far), when the training director finally ran down.

As soon as he was free, Henry called Hans.

"Henry! I've been trying to get you but you've been on your phone all morning!"

"I had a Costa Mango emergency. A Smithsonian staff member was being held captive."

"Is he free now?"

"Yes, thank God! What about the mummy?"

"We think we've found what we were looking for, but it isn't Kraft."

"Who is it?"

"We don't know, but we've done a carbon 14 dating on the windings and they are modern. I told Dr. Ossum to rip it open like it was Christmas morning, except that's not when we do it in Denmark. But he insists on opening it like it was a real Phaoronic mummy. He doesn't trust archaeometry. Says it's not science, it's conjuring mostly made up to give jobs to chemists. Anyway, when we X-rayed it we got a nice picture of some expensive bridgework and some teeth, but no dentures.

"Are you sure we have the right set of dental records for Kraft?

"They thought of that and checked it out. You've got to come up with a new name because if he really is mummified, he may not be easy to recognize. Depending on how good a job the murderer did, of course."

"Maybe he does it all the time and has had lots of practice.

Did Dr. Ossum have all the mummies checked, or did he stop when he found this one?"

"He went through the whole collection."

"Well, give me the news when Christmas morning gets here."

On impulse, Henry called Phoebe, who said she would be willing to have lunch as long as "that belly-dancer" wasn't along. So, newly light of heart, he was on his way down the steps. *62, 61, 60, 59, 58, 57, 56, 55,* turn at the landing, *54, 53.* "Is this the way to the Foreign Affairs Office?" asked the man who blocked his way.

"Damn! You made me lose count; I was doing it backward!"

"Sorry, old man, I'm looking for Henry Scruggs."

"That's all right, I'd probably have gotten mixed-up anyway. I'm Scruggs, what did you want? I'm going to lunch." Henry started easing past him in the narrow stairway.

"My name is Carl Harrison. I'm with the *Post.*"

"I'm under orders not to talk to you. Not you, specifically, but to any of the press." Henry had now gotten by him, so their positions were reversed.

"I don't see why, when we have everything from the police. Most of it's old news anyway. If you didn't keep finding bodies, it would be back on page six of Metro."

"Well, maybe I can give you some deep background off the record, but right now I'm keeping a lady waiting for lunch." Henry had, without appearing to move, made it down to the second landing. From there he could make a run for it and probably duck into the Office of Museum Programs before Harrison got to the bottom of the stairwell.

"I'll join you; I haven't eaten either."

Henry fled down the steps with Harrison hurrying after him. "You would get us both fired if we had lunch with you in the castle. Call me later."

"I'll take you to lunch someplace else."

"Both of us?" Henry stopped dead in his tracks.

Harrison caught up with him. "Both of you. Hammel's."

"No, people from Natural History eat there. We would

have to go somewhere people wouldn't see us. How about the Occidental?"

"That's kind of expen—oh, hell! Done!"

So it was that Henry and Phoebe went to lunch at the Occidental at the expense of the *Washington Post,* which could well afford it anyway.

"There's a third body?" asked Harrison, after he caught the drift of Henry and Phoebe's conversation. He had a mouthful of Cornish game hen.

"Yes, wrapped up and stacked with the mummies," replied Henry. "And papas, too, I suppose." Phoebe made a face at him.

"Who is it?"

"Well, we think it isn't Assistant Secretary Kraft," admitted Phoebe, who had also heard from Hans. "It doesn't have false teeth."

"Could it have been Mr. Kraft if it had have had false teeth?"

"Doctor," said Henry.

"Doctor, what about doctor?" asked Harrison, becoming more confused.

"Dr. Kraft," explained Phoebe, kindly. "The rule is a little bit complicated. Anybody who is a physician is a 'doctor,' but if you are a Ph.D., you are only a 'doctor' if you are not a gentleman. That's why it's 'Doctor' Kraft and 'Mister' Whitfield."

"Exactly," agreed Henry.

"What the hell has that got to do with the murders?"

"Why, nothing at all. We just want the *Post* to get everything right."

"God! Museum people! Nothing personal, of course," Harrison added quickly. "Why did you bring up 'Doctor' Kraft, if I've got it right?"

"Well, only because he's been missing for a month." Phoebe smiled nicely as she widened her mouth to pour in a third martini. She was paying little attention to her sautéed sole.

"But this new body you've found, whose is it?"

"It is only my opinion, of course, but I rather imagine it is Mr. Haley." Henry's tongue had been oiled with Scotch. Slower, perhaps, but in the long run just as effective as martinis.

"And who is Mr. Haley? Is 'Mister' right and not 'Doctor'? Does that mean he's a gentleman, whatever that is?"

"No, 'Mister' is perfectly correct because he doesn't have a Ph.D."

"Or an M.D., of course," added Henry. "Treasurers don't need them."

"The Smithsonian Treasurer? He's missing too?" Harrison put down his fork and reached for his spiral pad and ballpoint.

"We don't exactly know, but nobody's seen him for a long time. If he isn't dead, we ought to count our money, don't you think?" Phoebe held up her empty glass for a refill.

Henry and Phoebe didn't make it back to work that afternoon.

Since Henry always read the funnies and the obituaries at breakfast in the morning and got to the front section of the paper with his dinner in the evening, he missed seeing the headline across the top of page one of the *Washington Post* about the third Smithsonian murder. He particularly missed seeing himself given credit in the lead paragraph for discovering all the bodies. Assistant General Counsel Phoebe Casey was given credit for postulating a fourth murder. The *Post* had suppressed, probably at the last moment, the suggestion that Dr. Kraft might be the fourth victim.

Henry should have known something was amiss because there were sixty-four steps that morning and they felt like a hundred. He draped himself over the newel post at the top of the stairs until he felt he could go on. When he rounded the corner to enter his office he could see there were two strange shapes already sitting at his desk, one of them uniformed. The other one wore a seersucker suit as though it were a uniform and his revolver bulged under his armpit.

"Mr. Scruggs?" The seersucker suit held up a wallet open to a city detective's badge. "I'm Lieutenant Jones and this is Detective Sergeant Smith. We'd like you to come with us."

"Where to?" Henry sighed. He didn't believe for one moment their names were Smith and Jones.

"Down to police headquarters. We want to talk to you about the Smithsonian murders."

On the way, Henry sat in the back of the police car. The stiff springs and hard plastic upholstery did nothing for the delicate condition of his stomach.

At headquarters, Henry "spilled his guts" figuratively (and almost literally), which was all taken down and given to him to read. The inaccuracies were only minor, so he signed his name at the bottom, where it seemed to be required. "Can I go now?" he asked.

"We will tell you when you can go," said Lieutenant Jones. He led Henry to a small room with a chair and a light bulb and abandoned him there. Henry heard the door being locked.

He looked around the room. It wasn't exactly a jail cell, but it might just as well have been. The single light bulb was in a fixture mounted on the ceiling. There were no openings in the room except for two small air vents and the door. The door opened out so even the hinge pins were inaccessible. Henry thought that if they never came back for him he would just have to die. It would be the fifth Smithsonian murder, assuming they ever found Kraft's body.

Without thinking about it, Henry started counting the floor tiles. He kept losing his place so eventually he had to get up out of the chair and walk carefully from tile to tile, as he counted, in order to keep track. There were exactly 256 tiles at what looked to be nine inches square. He checked the number of tiles on each of two sides and calculated for a moment. The room was twelve feet square. He tried to calculate the number of square inches but he found he couldn't do it in his head and they had taken away his pen.

Henry paced slowly back and forth, mentally tracing an imaginary continuous line around each tile and avoiding going over any line twice (crossings were permitted) to see how many squares he could completely enclose. After a while it got very confusing and he became dizzy. He had to sit down.

He wound his watch every fifteen minutes. If it ran down, he would never be able to set it because there was no sun time or anything else to go by. He must remember to mark off twelve-hour segments somehow, otherwise he would lose track of night and day. He felt in his pocket. Ah! Good! He had lots of change. They hadn't taken that away. He supposed they had decided that change wasn't a weapon and he could be trusted with it. Or perhaps it was held to be un-American to take a prisoner's change so he couldn't use a vending machine.

He fished out a penny and placed it on one of the floor tiles in a corner of the room. That would mark the first twelve-hour period. At noon, in twenty-three minutes, he would have to remember to put out another coin. He felt his coins again. Good! Before he used them up he would be dead of thirst.

A while after placing the second coin, Henry became bored and started counting the floor tiles backwards: 256, 255, 254, 253, 252, 251, 250 . . .

It was three thirty-five, marked by the second period (a nickel), when they came to get him. Henry had been locked up for almost four hours and he had missed his lunch. He was going to hold Mayor Walter Washington personally responsible.

"Sit down, Mr. Scruggs. Is this your statement?" The unidentified man held up some papers for Henry to see.

"I don't know. I can't tell when you wave them at me like that."

"It's yours. Now tell us how long you've worked for the Smithsonian?"

"I work for the State Department. I'm on loan to the Smithsonian."

"You have an office in the Smithsonian?"

"Yes."

"You work there. How long?"

"Six months, almost seven."

"Why is it you seem to know where all the bodies are? Did you happen to see the murders committed?"

"No, of course not. Have they positively identified the third body yet?"

"We are asking the questions. How is it that you are able to find the bodies when they are hidden so well nobody else can?"

"I bring to the Smithsonian a refreshing, outside point of view."

"Cut out the bullshit. The paper this morning said you told them that the third body was Haley. How did you know that?

"I didn't know that. I only guessed. Nobody has seen Mr. Haley for weeks. It seemed reasonable that if a body turned up, it would be somebody who was missing."

"And you just happened to think he might be wrapped up like a mummy."

"Yes."

"What about Kraft?"

"It couldn't have been Kraft, it still had some teeth."

"Well, that certainly sounds perfectly reasonable," said the questioner sarcastically.

"I thought so."

"Where is Kraft, then?"

"I really don't know. But if you'll let me out of here, I might be able to figure it out."

The policeman was silent for a long time, then, "Okay. Okay, you can go now, but don't leave town. We'll be talking to you again."

It was late afternoon when Henry finally made it out onto the street. The restaurants were all closed, so he was reduced to going to a McDonald's. He secretly liked all the salt and grease in hamburgers and french fries. He topped it off with a chocolate shake and let out his belt one notch.

* * *

The next morning, Henry called Hans. There had been a meeting on the previous afternoon, which Henry had missed because of his session with the police. Yes, the body had been Mr. Haley. Not only had the dental records checked, but the body had been recognizable if you knew whom you were looking for. It had been grisly.

There was a note from the temporary secretary to call Tomlinson at IIE about another foreign visitor. It was marked urgent. Henry picked up his phone and dialed.

"Who is it this time? asked Henry.

"A general from the Brazilian Air Force. General Machado."

"And I suppose he wants to come over tomorrow. I don't know if I can get anybody to take him through that soon. A lot of the docents and curators are still on vacation."

"Not tomorrow, this afternoon."

"Huh? There's certainly no way I can get anybody today. He might just as well go through by himself."

"I thought you could do it."

Henry decided that someday he was going to have to go over to the IIE offices and have a little talk with the staff about the kinds of demands they placed on the Smithsonian and, more particularly, on him. If it went much further he would be working full time for the likes of Tomlinson and Saldana, providing filler for their Washington programs for State Department–sponsored visitors.

The rest of Henry's morning was taken up by a dressing-down administered by Ambassador Craddock. Henry explained that the *Post* reporter had gotten all the facts elsewhere (not true, of course) and had challenged him to deny them, which he could not do since he wasn't instructed to lie to the press. It was about as good a defense as he could come up with on short notice. Craddock exhibited no sympathy at all for Henry being the police's principal suspect.

"I've also heard from the Secretary!" said Craddock, as if that were something to be avoided at all costs.

"That's nice. I'm glad he's taking an interest in the murders. He hasn't attended any of our meetings."

"He was threatening to abolish this office! He particularly

101

wanted to know about the Kraft business, about his passport."

"I don't think Kraft will be needing it anymore. I think he's dead." Henry had not thought about this aspect of the Kraft affair, but now that he did, it seemed things had worked themselves out rather nicely.

"If I were still an ambassador and you were serving under me, I'd stick you off somewhere like the visa section."

"That's where I used to serve—in the visa section."

"That figures." Craddock knew it all along.

Lunch was a high spot on an otherwise dreary day in a less-than-perfect week. Henry had his lunch with Phoebe in the Commons. The room was atwitter with speculation. A growing number of their colleagues were betting that they were co-conspirators in mass murder. Almost no one, except possibly the murderer, would have staked his life that Henry was uninvolved.

"Habeas Corpus bawled me out. He made a bunch of sexist remarks. Did you get it too?"

"The same. Except Craddock made anti-consular service remarks. It's just like sexism except if you're a woman as well as being a consul, then it is twice as bad, I guess."

"Do you think anybody will hire us after we get fired?"

"We're not going to get fired. We're going to solve the case."

"If we're going to do that, we'd better get started, Henry." Phoebe looked doubtful.

"I think we're agreed that Bill of Rights was probably killed in the Castle and carried over to Natural History through the tunnel. Then I think the murderer cut him up in one of the exhibits labs on the south side of the basement and took the body, piece by piece, up the iron steps to the freeze-dry equipment. When he was all nicely dehydrated and frozen he must have been brought back the same way to the Castle and placed in the sarcophagus. The Smithson bones were removed the same way and hidden in Physical Anthropology. That was actually the most trouble because it required going up to the third floor of the Natural History Museum and across to the other side of the building."

"We don't know when," Phoebe reminded Henry, "and I don't know why you think Mr. Wright had to have been killed in the Castle."

"Two reasons. General Counsels seldom go wandering around the museums after hours, and even if Wright had done so, there would have been enough people working odd hours in Natural History that he would have been noticed. I think he visited Natural History in a specimen cart. I like the Castle for murders because it is usually deserted after hours. Besides, it's spooky."

"I must remember to take my extra work home with me," said Phoebe uncomfortably. "I suppose Percy Jammers could have been killed in the Castle, too, but I don't think so."

"I think I agree with you, but I'd like to hear your reasons."

"Percy would have to have been gotten out back of the Castle to the beetle shed somehow. The most direct route would have been the south basement door, but that is locked up tight at six o'clock. Besides there would be a guard on it when it was open. Percy had to have been killed out by the shed or maybe the parking lot."

"I thought," said Henry, "about taking him up on top of the south tower and lowering him from the battlements, but your way makes more sense. And after he was eaten, getting his remains from the beetle shed to the Natural History building would have been simple."

"I don't see why. The tunnel only runs between the Castle and the Museum of Natural History. Everything going in or out of the Castle gets inspected. Even my briefcase. The guards don't look into my purse, but they would if it were big enough for a skeleton."

"If I were the murderer, I would simply write a work order and have the labor force take the bones to Physical Anthropology."

Phoebe admired the simplicity of that, but she had two

objections: "You would still have a property pass and you would have to sign the work order. If the murder did as you suggest, we would only have to look at the completed work orders to find out who it is."

"We probably ought to do that but it wouldn't necessarily be of any help. You could sign anybody's name to a work order. And as far as the property pass is concerned, you wouldn't need a pass to get the bones out of the shed because there's no security there and you don't need a pass to get things into Natural History or any of the other public buildings of the Smithsonian. The guards never even look into things like specimen boxes. You could hide an atom bomb in one if you could carry it."

"Then there's the third murder," said Phoebe. "I suppose that Mr. Haley could have been handled the same way as Mr. Wright?"

"Transporting the bodies within the Castle gives me some problems for both Wright and Haley. The east elevator is the only one that goes high enough to reach the General Counsel's office and it passes right by the guard station. The guard could look right in the glass door."

"The murderer could have brought Wright down from the fourth floor to the third in the east elevator and then changed to the front elevator to go from the third floor to the basement. That way he wouldn't have been anywhere near the guard station. The Treasurer's office is on the third, so the front elevator would have been fine for him. The principal problem would be carrying bodies down those long corridors. I suppose it wouldn't be a problem if the murderer were really strong." Phoebe looked uncomfortable at the thought of terribly strong murderers lurking about the Castle.

"I couldn't do it," said Henry who didn't, however, regard himself as particularly strong. "I think I would use a swivel chair. You could get one in almost any office. The only danger would be the guards' shift change time, because the guards' dressing room is on the same basement corridor as the tunnel entrance. Even an off-duty guard might notice you trundling along a corpse in an office chair."

"It must take a while to mummify somebody. How would you do that? I don't even like to clean fish." Phoebe made a face.

"You would have to pick the laboratory of somebody away on a long field trip. Vertebrate Zoology, I should think. You could keep the body under rags soaked in formalin while you were working on it. Only the cleaning people would come near it and I feel reasonably sure they wouldn't touch it."

"That makes some sort of grisly sense," said Phoebe. "Now, we have to find Dr. Kraft. And we have to figure who the murderer is."

"Before we decide who the murder is, I think there is something perhaps more important we have to discover."

"What is that, Henry?" Phoebe set herself immediately to thinking about another person who might be missing.

"Why? Why did the murderer do it?"

"Oh! We haven't thought much about that, have we?"

"No, and until we know why, we will always be at least a step behind the murderer."

"Perhaps somebody doesn't like the Executive Committee."

"No, Jammers was only an office director. The Executive Committee only goes down as far as the assistant secretaries. But I think it was more selective than that. Every victim was a member of the IPES review committee."

"I don't see the connection. We don't know for sure about Dr. Kraft. And nothing has happened to Dr. Haas."

"Yet."

General Machado turned out not to be just any old air force general but Vice Chief of Staff. He took it with wry Brazilian good grace that no one more important than Henry had received him at the Smithsonian. He took it calmly that most of the famous Smithsonian aircraft collection was in storage awaiting the construction of the new museum. He walked in the front door of the Arts and Industries Building and stopped and looked up at the Wright Flyer.

"At last," he said, "you admit it."

Henry followed his gaze. When he had shown it to Dr. Kunjeer, he had not really looked at it. He had seen it a hundred times, perhaps, until he quit noticing it, quit paying it any attention, but there was the actual airplane that launched manned flight at Kitty Hawk in 1903. A dummy of one of the Wrights was at the controls. Henry was not sure whether it was supposed to be Orville or Wilbur. "I don't understand," he said.

"It is not the first airplane to fly. The first was built by Santos Dumont, the great Brazilian," General Machado said proudly. "And now you have placed a number two on the Wright airplane. The United States is a great country to admit it is second best."

Henry saw what the general meant. Affixed to the Flyer was a card with the number 2. The museum staff put it on (over the objection of the curator) to key the Flyer (the second exhibit as you came in the entrance, the unsuccessful Langley airplane being the first) to the headphone and tape player you could rent at the door to explain the exhibits. "The Smithsonian could do no less," Henry replied. "I'm sure in Brazil you admit we were first on the moon."

They went on to see the Bell XP-1, the Goddard rockets, and the Apollo 11, and the other space hardware. Then they turned into the just opened and already Henry's personal favorite among the aircraft exhibits, the mockup of a forward airstrip in World War I France. Two short-nosed, French-built Spads of Eddie Rickenbacker's Hat-in-the-Ring Squadron were stunting in the air over the field and a perfect and perfectly beautiful Fokker D-7 was on the ground, illustrating an incident when a German flyer landed on the field, thinking it was in German hands, and was captured by the Allies. In a shed on the edge of the tiny field stood a wonderful German Albatross, all bright and beautifully varnished wood.

Henry stood below and admired the pair of Spads once

again. The Wright Flyer got boring after a while, but these three airplanes were forever a pleasure. Up above him a dummy of Eddie, wearing goggles and helmet, looked back down at the general and at Henry standing on the field. Rickenbacker was still alive, Henry believed. He wondered if the old man had seen this exhibit. Did he think the dummy looked like him? Of course he would think so. The way it was dressed, it could look like anybody, even Dr. Kraft.

As Henry took General Machado outside to see the exhibits in the hangar building, he was distracted and heard little of what the general said. Over and over in his mind turned the thought of Dr. Kraft riding up to heaven in a Spad.

Henry was awake all night. What had begun as only a flight, so to speak, of imagination, was taking on the smell of certainty. He was in his office at the ridiculously early hour of 9:30 A.M. and called Phoebe at once. He would have called her at 3:00 A.M. except that her home phone number wasn't listed. The Office of General Counsel was having a staff meeting and the receptionist said she would have Phoebe call as soon as she got out. Henry knew better than to trust that his message would be delivered. He put down the phone and went down the steps, *62, 60, 58,* jump three to the landing, *53, 51 . . .*

The staff meeting went on forever. He could hear Bodde droning on and on about how everybody was going to have to work harder now that Mr. Wright was gone. How many ways where there that he could say it? Phoebe and everybody else but Bodde got more and more fidgety. If she turned her head only a little bit more, she would be able to see Henry outside the open door. Henry stared at her. He had found that if you looked at a woman long enough, she was bound to notice it. He concentrated. Eventually just about everybody else in the room had turned around and was staring at Henry. Phoebe, however, was not. Perhaps she was just used to being looked at. Somebody, Henry couldn't see who, got up and closed the door.

Lunchtime arrived and still the door had not opened.

Could they have brought box lunches? Surely somebody would eventually have to leave to go to the bathroom. Henry waited.

At 12:47 the door was yanked open and people poured out of the conference room. Henry jumped back to keep from being trampled. "Have lunch with me!" he shouted to Phoebe. She looked at him curiously. "I think I know where Kraft is!"

It was the worst time to go to the Commons. They had to wait for a table and Phoebe badgered Henry to give her a hint. Everybody in the line got suddenly quiet so they could hear. "He's tied up in the clock tower. He was driven mad by the sound of the bells."

"That's stupid. The clock doesn't have any bells."

"No, maybe you're right. It was the sound of the carousel. That would do it." People went back to their own conversations. They agreed with Phoebe.

Henry bent close to Phoebe's ear. She tilted her head to hear what he had to whisper. He closed his mouth over her ear. It had looked delicious.

In the confusion the maître d' called them. Their table was ready.

Several times people started to approach them to speak and then thought better of it.

"If they knew what I think I know, they'd run for cover."

"Tell!" demanded Phoebe. She was only half-convinced that Henry really had something to say and had not just been trying to get her into the Commons for God-knows-what.

"Eddie Rickenbacker. Dr. Kraft is Eddie Rickenbacker."

"Eddie Rickenbacker is dead. He's got to be by now."

"No, he's not. I've checked."

"He's a very old man."

"He is that."

"Dr. Kraft is a dirty man but he's not that old."

"I don't mean the old Eddie Rickenbacker, I mean the young one. The dummy in the Spad."

"The dummy?"

"That's where he is. He's the dummy."

"That's impossible."

"I don't see why."

"He'd have to be preserved. He's too big to freeze-dry. You'd notice it if the beetles ate his flesh up. And you could also tell if he had been mummified. That's why it's impossible."

"There's another way."

"Tell me what it is," she demanded.

"I don't know. There's just got to be one. It is up to us to figure it out."

After a forgettable and forgotten lunch, they stood in the A&I Building, on the World War I forward airstrip in France, and looked up at the Spad. "That's got to be John Armour Kraft. Jack Armstrong, the all-American pilot."

It had to be true. Phoebe squeezed Henry's hand with excitement.

Nine

After Henry got back to his office (sixty-two steps and holding) he had his usual call from IIE. This time there were two visits, an American studies teacher from the Philippines and two officials from the Singapore Science Center. The lady from the Philippines, Henry agreed to see on Tuesday, but he put the gentlemen from Singapore off until Wednesday because the arrangements were more complicated.

Tea was served at three-fifteen. Again there were no Fig Newtons, but Dreamy Weekes had brought in brownies that she had made from chocolate truffles and marijuana. Ronald Hipster proposed marriage to Dreamy on the spot. She turned him down. Actually, she said she would have to ask her husband, which was the same thing. Henry took advantage of the attention the exchange attracted to swipe two more brownies. Henry was seen, however, by Sally who raised hell as only she could do it. Henry was forced by Ambassador Craddock to give one back.

When order was restored, Henry brought up an item of business. It was not entirely to distract attention from his shameful gluttony. He also thought it was a good idea to spend a few minutes discussing business because otherwise Ambassador Craddock might decide that the two-hour afternoon teatime was not fitting for the dignity of a foreign affairs office in a renowned public institution. Especially in view of the Secretary's threat to abolish the office.

"Mr. Ambassador, I want to set up an American studies meeting on Tuesday morning. There's a woman coming from the Philippines who is head of American studies at the Evangelista y Marcos Teacher's College. It would be appropriate if you were to preside."

Craddock looked uncomfortable and Henry could see he was trying to think of some way to get out of it, so he let him off the hook. "Of course the meeting might last for a while and if you have other pressing commitments, perhaps Ronald could represent you." Craddock should remember that kindness when it came time for him to turn in Henry's efficiency report to the State Department.

"I'm sure Mr. Hipster could contribute a lot to the meeting," Craddock said with transparent relief.

"I don't know, Steub." That's what Ronald always said when asked to do anything, and his familiar contraction of Craddock's first name always made Henry cringe. Henry could not even bring himself to call his boss "Steuben." It wasn't the proper way for a Southerner to address someone of an earlier generation, let alone a former ambassador.

"I'm told she is very beautiful," Henry lied, knowing one of Ronald's many weak points.

"Why, sure." Ronald shifted to bleary interest. "What would you like me to talk about?"

"Nothing in particular. Just preside. I'll see if I can get Hamilton Sealyham to attend and maybe Taylor Maidstone. Taylor is mostly South Asian, but I think he has done some American urban anthropology. Of course Hamilton can talk about anything. If Dr. Ezra Fairburn isn't tied up in one of his American Studies seminars, I'll get him too."

Henry cut short his teatime partly because Dreamy had left the office early and it was kind of dull talking to the men and Sally, but mostly because he wanted to telephone Hamilton before he left his office.

Hamilton said he'd be delighted to perform on Tuesday, and that he'd bring Taylor who was, even as they spoke, sitting across the desk discussing the possibility of an after-work drink. Or two. *"Why don't you join us Mr. Foreign Secretary? You might bring along Miss Casey."* Hamilton's thirst for gossip was obvious.

Henry agreed and called Phoebe, who started, reflexively, to say no and then changed her mind when she thought about something happening that she might miss. Then, Henry called Fairburn at the American Studies Office in the Museum of American History, but nobody answered his phone. He would have to try again on Monday.

Henry was back at the teapot pouring the tepid dregs of now strong tea into his cup when the Under Secretary called and summoned him to the Castle. He hurried over, taking steps two at a time—*62, 60, 58, 56, 54,* the landing, *53, 51* . . . If he got there fast enough, perhaps he could finish up with Mr. Owens and still catch up with the drinks crowd.

Secretary Whitfield was sitting in on of the chairs in the Under Secretary's office. Henry was startled. This was something that hadn't happened before. "Please sit down Mr. Scruggs, we were just talking about recent events."

"Yes, sir. Good evening, Mr. Secretary." Henry remembered as he sat down that people up here in Washington don't say "good evening" for any time between lunch and nightfall the way they do down home. Perhaps they'll think he is trying to be sarcastic about such a late-in-the day meeting. However, that might be all to the good.

"Mr. Scruggs," said Secretary Whitfield, "you have let several days go by without finding any more bodies. Are there to be any more? If so, we should very much like to hear it before we learn about it in the newspapers."

"One, I think. Or possibly two."

"Explain yourself," demanded the Under Secretary.

"I can't. At least not entirely. It's just a feeling I have. Dr. Kraft doesn't seem to be accounted for, and I believe if I think about it enough, I might be able to discover where he is. Or his remains are, rather. It also seems to me that the murderer might not be finished yet."

"What Mr. Owens and I would like to hear," said the

Secretary, "is what you think you know, even if you don't have proof."

"That is just the point. What I think I know is simply impossible. If I could find out how it is possible, then I would feel that I could tell people and it could be investigated. As it is, people would think I was being silly."

"Your record for finding bodies so far has been phenomenal, rather than silly," observed the Under Secretary. "Sort of like a hound trained to sniff out truffles."

"Pigs actually do it better, I believe," suggested Secretary Whitfield.

Henry let any possible invidious interpretation of that remark pass. "I have been lucky. Or unlucky, considering the suspicions of the police. But I don't want to face them again until I have something better to go on."

"When you think you know something, I want you to come to me directly." said Secretary Whitfield, "or in the event I'm not available, to Mr. Owens. Is that clear?"

"Yes, sir. Is that all, sir?" Henry had sneaked a look at his watch and was ready, in fact eager, to leave.

"There is one other thing," said Secretary Whitfield and nodded to the Under Secretary.

"Yes," agreed the Under Secretary. "I asked you to look into the IPES operations."

"Yes, sir! I'm sorry I haven't gotten very far with it. A lot of other things have come up, not to mention the murders. But I have been out to Anacostia once for a look-around and I plan to get in deeper next week." Henry felt like he was back in school and had been caught not doing his homework. It was hardly fair considering that no deadline had been mentioned.

"The Secretary thinks you should drop it for the time being. It may be inappropriate for you to study the operation in view of the work already done by the IPES committee. At any rate, I have one other thing I want you to do next week. I would like you to get messages out to our people working abroad to verify their whereabouts."

Henry said, sure, he could do that. He would have to get

113

copies of all the travel orders so he would know where to look for people abroad, but it ought to be possible. Henry got up to leave before they thought of something else to talk about.

"Oh, Mr. Scruggs!" Secretary Whitfield called as Henry was about to go out the door."

"Yes, sir?"

"Better keep your head down. It appears that Mr. Haley was garrotted. There were marks on the mummy."

Phoebe was waiting impatiently when Henry climbed the steps to her office at a run. *(2, 4, 6, 8, 10, the landing, 12, 14 . . .)* "Sorry, I'm late! Let's go, we can catch up with the others."

Usually, when Henry walked across the Mall and when the damned calliope wasn't playing, he tried to maintain a pace of 120 per minute unless he was tired, and then sometimes it dropped to about 111. He peeked at his watch. Phoebe was doing less than 100. Oh, well! She had other qualities.

It took eighteen minutes to make it to the bar at the Hotel Washington. That's like forever if you need a drink. Hamilton and Taylor were already settled at a table and had been served.

"We wondered whether you two had decided to go off by yourselves," Taylor's eyes raked Phoebe, top to bottom. She hurriedly sat down to minimize her exposure, particularly her leather miniskirt, which had proved to be shorter than it had appeared when she had tried it on in the store.

"I had an unexpected meeting with Mr. Whitfield and Mr. Owens."

"Considering the number of bodies around, that almost constituted a quorum of the Executive Committee. Has anything new happened? Has the Smithsonian Slaughterer struck again?" Hamilton rolled his eyes in mock horror. Truth to tell he had never enjoyed himself so much in his life, not even when studying the last of the head-shrinking cannibals.

"That's what they wanted to know, but I didn't have anything new to tell them. I did, however, mention my hope to be able to turn up Dr. Kraft's body and I suggested there might be another one."

"What is this about another body?" demanded Phoebe. She had been ordering her drink and suddenly returned her attention to the conversation.

"You know, Phoebe, what we were talking about yesterday in the Commons."

"Oh, that one."

Henry explained to Hamilton and Taylor, "It is a question of . . . missing numbers."

"Numbers of what?"

"All the known victims are members of a committee."

"Kraft too? What committee?"

"Kraft too. And there is one other member on the committee. Dr. Haas, in the Library. It's the committee studying publications exchanges."

"Then Dr. Haas might become another victim?" Taylor smiled, baring his teeth, hungrily. Hamilton's face drained of color.

"Or she might be the murderer. And I should have said that there might be three murders to discover."

"Who is the third?" asked Taylor.

"Me." Henry took his glass of Scotch from the waitress. He smiled at her, and then at his companions in the silence that followed.

Henry continued his presentation. "You see, from what we now know, there are two possible scenarios, three actually, for the murders and they both contain the same kind of flaw. In the beginning, Hamilton, I favored you and Taylor as a conspiracy to commit murder. You both have reasons to get rid of Kraft, Jammers, and the Treasurer. They aren't reasons that would drive most people to murder, but I think they are good enough for you."

"Why, certainly! These so-called victims only brought it on themselves! I must admit I have toyed with the idea," agreed Hamilton.

115

"It would only have been a matter of time," Taylor confirmed.

"Did you commit the murders?"

"No, no! Of course not, dear boy. It was unnecessary to do so. Someone else did them before we could get around to it. Naturally I only speak for myself. You didn't do it, did you, Taylor?"

"No, of course not. You see Henry, the blood is only on our thoughts, not our hands."

"I thought not. I couldn't see why you would also kill Bill of Rights, unless it was some petty, personal grudge I didn't know about. Or perhaps just to obscure your motive for killing the others."

"Oh, we would never do that!" Taylor said with only a tinge of insincerity.

"Now, on the other hand, everyone who has been killed, including Kraft, who has probably been killed, served on the IPES study committee. It might seem that someone wants the committee out of the way, except that Dr. Haas is also on the committee and she has not been harmed."

"Of course," added Phoebe, "she might be the murderer. Or she might be the next victim."

"Oh dear, oh dear, oh dear!" said Hamilton. "I suppose we should either warn her or warn everybody else about her." He expressed the depth of his concern by hunting around in the potato chip bowl for something better than the predominating crumbs. He found a bit of salt and licked his fingers. Taylor watched him while he waited for Henry to go on.

"When Mr. Owens asked me to look into IPES, he may have added my name to the murderer's list. Interestingly, Dr. Haas tried to intimidate me into staying away from IPES. And now Secretary Whitfield has called me off. That was one of the things he wanted to talk to me about this afternoon. It is possible, I suppose, that Dr. Haas got him to do it so she wouldn't have to murder me."

"I doubt it," said Taylor. "That Haas is a cold-hearted

116

woman. I don't think she'd mind adding your blood to the others."

"Who is the other, Henry?" asked Phoebe, who was keeping track.

"What other?"

"The other possible murderer. You said there were three."

"Oh! That's me. Some people seem to think I did it. Kraft, at least, wanted to get rid of me."

"Did you do it, Henry? You can tell me; I won't tell anybody," said Taylor, as might be expected.

"I covered my tracks," answered Henry enigmatically.

"How do you plan to proceed now?" Hamilton was showing his rare practical side, a sure sign he had had too much to drink.

"The first thing we need to do is to figure out how to preserve Kraft's body as a museum display dummy."

"Is that what I did with the body? I had forgotten," said Taylor.

"That is what the murderer probably did," said Phoebe. "That is his style, his M.O."

"Or her, Miss Casey."

"Oh, I suppose so, Hamilton, but all this is a big order for a sweet, delicate female."

"What we need is a fourth way to deal with the decomposition of a body. The murderer doesn't appear to be repeating herself on successive murders."

"Or himself," said Phoebe.

"Anyway, I think that if there is a fourth way to preserve the body, we will find it riding in a Spad and pretending to be Eddie Rickenbacker."

"Now that would be a good place for Kraft. He was rather a dummy in life, so why shouldn't he become one in death. Don't you agree, Hamilton?"

"Well, if you think Kraft could learn his lines, Taylor, I suppose it would be type-casting." Hamilton and Taylor nodded their heads in agreement with one another.

"But how could it be done?" persisted Henry.

117

"If you didn't insist on putting him in a flimsy little airplane, I suppose he could be bronzed like baby shoes. Then he could be stood up in a diorama in the Natural History Museum. 'Early man, searching for his mate.'" Taylor looked pleased with his idea. "Of course, he would have to be naked. All our exhibits are naked. There may be people around here who would recognize Kraft that way, I just don't know."

"I think more probably Dr. Kraft would be looking for his link." Phoebe smiled at the thought.

"Bronzing anything that big would be rather difficult," said Hamilton, who knew a little bit about everything, "and the body would probably have to be sent off to Italy or someplace. I favor a plain plaster covering."

"That's been done several times in fiction," said Phoebe, who read murder mystery stories, "and I think our murderer is more imaginative than that."

"Well that's the problem I'm working on, or at least will be after I have another drink." If Henry did resume working on the problem that day, he was not conscious of it.

It was late morning when Henry awoke. At first, he was disoriented and then he decided he must be in a hotel. He must be in a hotel with a hangover, one big enough to require a double bed. Or so it felt. He could hear a shower running. It sounded a bit like being directly under Niagara Falls. It drummed into his skull, eroding the bone. After three days of eternity had passed, the shower was cut off and in the shocking silence that followed, there came the sort of moving-about sounds associated with drying off and getting dressed. A small body, he decided. It had to be a small body being dried and dressed.

He felt under the sheet. No clothes there. It must be his body in the bed, but it felt as though it belonged to someone else. Henry squinted his eyes so he could see better without his glasses. A pile of something that looked like his clothes was in a chair, well out of reach. It looked haloed from the blinding light of the window beyond it.

Henry extended his hand over to the other side of the bed, the one reserved for his hangover. There was a warm depression there. Henry was not surprised. His hangover felt hot and solid. A billet of iron not yet cooled from the furnace. Phoebe came out of the bath, fully dressed, or as much so as possible considering her leather skirt. Henry cursed himself for oversleeping.

"You better hurry. It is almost checkout time."

It was a bitter-sweet-bitter weekend. Or at least it was after the effects of Friday evening's intemperate drinking wore off. It was bitter because Henry was unable to get Phoebe back into a hotel room or any other kind of bedroom. But it was sweet because she seemed content with his company elsewhere. For the first time since Henry had returned from abroad, he did not feel lonely on a weekend.

It was also bitter because it was mid-September and the ragweed and Henry's nose were coming into flower. It came to him, with an odd sense of surprise, that he had forgotten to limit his drinking when he began taking antihistamines this season. That was careless of him. And dangerous.

The second day after the Ides of September dawned a perfect day—at least for those who did not suffer from hay fever—cool, dry, and clear with clean Canadian air. Henry had found it necessary to take a pill in the middle of the night and again in the morning to dry up his nose. Then he had lingered rather long over tea to wake himself up.

They were assembled in the FAO conference room when Henry arrived. He hadn't hurried, but had climbed and counted the steps leisurely because Ronald Hipster was supposed to be running the meeting. And anyway, all those American studies people had been invited to talk to the lady from the Philippines and they could do it very well without Henry.

He peeked into the conference room. Hamilton, Taylor, and Dr. Fairburn were all there and Fairburn was speaking. The woman he was addressing was truly beautiful. Henry

119

had not lied to Ronald Hipster. But Ronald was not there to appreciate it. "Where is Mr. Hipster?" Henry asked the new temporary receptionist, a lady in her forties (Henry's age, now that he thought about it, which he hadn't at the moment), widowed, divorced, bored, or children in college, making her way back into the labor force.

"Do you have an appointment, sir?" she asked.

"No, I'm Scruggs. I work here."

"Oh! Sorry, sir!" She was very embarrassed. It must be her first assignment with the temporary service. "I am Mrs. Plumm. Mr. Hipster called. He said he would be in soon. He said he was walking to work."

"Walking? He lives in Rockville!"

"I don't know, sir, he just said it was a beautiful morning so he was walking to work."

"Herr Gott!" said Henry.

"I beg your pardon?"

"I cursed. I usually do it in German."

"Why is that, may I ask?" She was becoming interested. Henry decided she had a nice smile but hadn't used it in a long time.

"I don't know French."

Henry apologized to the lady from the Philippines and his colleagues and sat down at the table, trying to look alert and interested, but the antihistamines were acting like a general anesthetic. He was drifting off to sleep when Mrs. Plumm stuck her head through the door to the conference room and made a hissing noise at Henry. He jumped.

Henry followed her into the outer office. "Mr. Hipster is on the phone. I told him you would like to speak to him."

Bright lady, thought Henry, this is one we ought to keep if we ever get a permanent slot. "Hello, Ronald?"

"Henry, old man! How are you this morning?"

"I might be better if you were here running the American studies meeting. Where are you?"

"I'm having breakfast. It is a perfect day, a joyous day, and I'm walking to work."

"From Rockville?"

"I'm not in Rockville now. I'm somewhere on Route 355. It's lovely out here. You would enjoy it, Henry. It would do you a world of good."

"My nose would run worse than it does now. When will you be here?"

"In a little while. Oh, here comes my breakfast, I have to hang up" [click].

Henry went back to the meeting. He resented it, because he had planned to get back to his survey of overseas research today. Handling files was the best way to keep awake. And if he failed to do so, he could at least sleep comfortably in his highback leather desk chair. Still, the Philippine lady was nice to look at. Perhaps he could stay awake by weaving elaborate sexual fantasies around her. He would start by unbuttoning her blouse.

Henry took his time, his fingers exploring her body before and after each article of clothing was removed. As he worked, he poured a whispered monologue of lust into her ear as his tongue caressed it. He was having problems with the catch on her garter belt (assuming she was wearing one) when Mrs. Plumm appeared at the door again.

"It's Mr. Hipster again," she said. "This time he wants to talk to you."

"Hello, Ronald? This is Henry."

"Hello, Henry. I'm sorry I was so abrupt with you when we spoke earlier, but my eggs and sausage came and you know how eggs are when they get cold. Wouldn't want to ruin a perfect day over something like that. Did you have anything else you wanted to say?"

"Where are you now, Ronald?" asked Henry, though he suspected he knew the answer.

"I'm having another breakfast. This weather does wonders for your appetite. But I'm getting lots of exercise, so it's all right."

"What is it now, hot cakes?"

"Exactly so! I wish you could have some with me. It's a perfect morning for them! Well, here comes the waitress. She's really stacked, Henry. So are the hot cakes!" Ronald chuckled good-humoredly.

"Don't hang up, Ronald. That reminds me to tell you that the lady from the Philippines is absolutely beautiful. I knew she was going to be pretty, but nothing like this! You should see her. You might want to take a bus so you can get here before she goes."

"I'll think about it, Henry, but I'm really enjoying the walk. Maybe you could ask her to wait for me?"

Ronald's third breakfast call came at one o'clock. Henry had already gone to the Commons for lunch with the guests, the lady from the Philippines now being reduced to a pair of high-heel pumps and a white camellia in her hair that Henry added for contrast with her hair's black luster. He was thinking about exchanging the camellia for a pure red rose. While he was at it he might just tattoo a butterfly on her (imagined) flawless left buttock.

Henry spent the afternoon dressing the Philippine lady. What with all the touching and giggling that went on, it was almost as much fun as the morning had been.

It was teatime and the American studies people had been gone almost an hour when Ronald Hipster arrived. As she had left, the Philippine lady had given Henry a rather odd look, leaving him to wonder whether she might not be just a wee bit telepathic. He hoped, if she were, that she had not taken it at all personally.

Henry was contemplating Dreamy Weekes as he drank his tea and wondering what it would be like to keep awake by removing the skimpy bits and pieces she wore. He saw she was aware he was looking at her and had figured out the drift if not the details of his thoughts. She ran her tongue around her lips. Ostensibly, it was to pick up any remaining crumbs of Fig Newtons (Henry had brought in a new supply), but she, and Henry thought he, knew the real reason she had taken her tongue out for an airing. Damn! thought Henry. She's a telepath. He wondered how he could turn that to his advantage.

He shifted his gaze away from Dreamy and it alighted on Ronald. Ronald had climbed all but the last few steps and was standing on number 57 or 58. He was looking pleased. He was in fact looking like a very large little boy, if you didn't notice there was only half of him extended above the stairs. Craddock's gaze followed Henry's. "Come on up, Hipster. We've been expecting you."

"Since this morning," said Dreamy, turning around.

Ronald climbed the rest of the way up to the tower level and stood there looking tired but happy. He had on pants that had once been white but were now mostly green. Grass stains, obviously. "I walked to work," he said proudly.

"You look like you crawled," said Sally disapprovingly.

Ronald looked down at his pants. "I had to cut across country and there wasn't any sidewalk. My wife will be mad at me. Uh, could I have some tea?"

Ten

The wind changed and it began to rain during the night, continuing into Wednesday. It was unseasonably cool and cloudy, and a light drizzle came into Washington from the Atlantic. Everybody was grumpy except for Henry and a few thousand other hay fever sufferers. Henry came up the steps, two at a time, *54*, the landing, *56, 58, 60,* and *62,* alert and ready to go to work on his foreign research survey. "Good morning, Mrs. Plumm!"

"Oh, Mr. Scruggs! There are some gentlemen waiting for you at the guard desk. I believe they're from Singapore."

Henry had forgotten. But no matter, it was a lovely day to be outside, taking foreign guests here and there. He turned around and *60, 58, 56,* the landing, *54. . . .*

Doctors Cheong and Goh were waiting patiently, looking up at the Wright Flyer that Mr. Wright—Orville or Wilbur, Henry was never sure—brought in for a landing that cold December day at Kitty Hawk. Weather Henry would have loved. "Sorry to keep you waiting. I had to stop by to see the Secretary of State this morning," Henry lied.

"Isn't he in London?" asked Dr. Goh.

"That's the Secretary. Did I say I called on the Secretary? It was the Assistant Secretary." Henry didn't say which assistant secretary, hoping Dr. Goh would leave it at that. Henry looked at his watch. It was already ten-seventeen, but no matter.

"We are scheduled to visit the Conservation Analytical Laboratory in the Museum of History and Technology at ten and the processing laboratory at the Museum of Natural History at eleven-thirty. Then I thought we'd have lunch in the staff dining room in the Commons." If the thought of food wouldn't distract Mr. Goh, considering his roly-poly well-fed look, then nothing would.

They set out at a brisk pace for the History and Technology Building, while Henry rather breathlessly explained the history of the Smithsonian and how it evolved into ten museums (albeit some not yet open, and as many as thirteen depending on what you chose to count as a museum), a zoo, an observatory, a tropical research institute, and other research and research-support units too numerous to mention, though Henry made a good beginning at it until he felt his guests' attention wandering.

"On the staff, we have 284 scientists, 113 scholars in history and the arts, 976 technicians, and 47 engineers, attorneys, and accountants," he continued.

"So many?" commented Dr. Cheong.

"I know, it seems like too many, doesn't it?"

Doctors Cheong (the thin one) and Goh (the fat one) were members of a government of Singapore commission overseeing the establishment of a natural history wing in their new National Science Museum. Their particular reason for visiting the Smithsonian was to learn about the conservation of organic collections in museums. People from Singapore, Henry had noticed, always had a serious purpose when they traveled, a bit like the Germans and unlike those from many other lands who simply wanted to have a good time and do only enough business to justify the trip.

Of course there were those such as Mrs. Ferro y Silva, who had something more basic in mind.

Most of the individual Smithsonian museums had one or more conservation departments, but the Conservation Analytical Laboratory, which happened to be located in the building with the Museum of History and Technology, served the whole institution, advising the museums and conducting research on particular conservation problems, such as bronze decay, dry rot in wood, deacidification of paper, and an unending number of other problems that plague the objects collected in museums and kept forever.

The gentlemen from Singapore were interested in everything and made copious notes with gold fountain pens in little notebooks. It was after eleven-fifteen when Henry was finally able to drag them away and head toward the Museum of Natural History, walking briskly.

In the Anthropology Processing Laboratory, one of the specialized conservation departments, they saw ancient basketry being repaired, broken pots reassembled, dyed materials being cleaned, squashed specimens being reshaped, and the like. Then they moved on to see how the collections were stored.

From there, they went to visit the disinfestation chamber where organic materials are treated to kill insects before they are brought into the museum. It was down in the basement next to the Radiation Physics Laboratory. The disinfestation chamber, was a small room, but large enough to walk into. "The chamber is isolated from the rest of the museum. We bring organic specimens directly in from the loading dock to the chamber on a dolly," the technician explained, "and then seal the chamber."

"Then do you put in the poison gas?" asked Dr. Cheong.

"No, first we have to pull a vacuum in the chamber. Then we pump in the gas to replace the air. That way the gas penetrates the material. Unless you use a vacuum, the gas only gets to the surface of the specimens and doesn't bother the bugs deep inside."

"What do you do with the gas?" asked Dr. Goh.

"After the gas has had time to kill the insects, we purge the chamber with air and the gas is exhausted out a stack mounted on the roof of the museum. It dissipates."

"Does it kill any birds?" asked Henry, whose mind was not on birds but racing ahead to the Smithsonian murders.

"Only if they sit on the stack. But the Ornithology Division made us put an ultrasonic whistle on the stack to scare off the birds before we empty the chamber."

At lunch, Henry was rather distracted. Here was a vacuum chamber big enough for a whole man if only you could figure out how to freeze-dry the victim while you exhausted the moisture in his body by means of the vacuum chamber. He would have to think about it after the gentlemen from Singapore departed. When the waitress came around to offer desserts, Henry realized that it had been some time since he had participated in the discussions at the luncheon table. He forced himself to rejoin the conversation, but found that in the absence of his attention they had begun speaking Chinese.

That evening Henry demanded Phoebe's company. "I have to talk to somebody," he explained.

"So you picked me," she said with the beginning of a pout.

"You're the only one I'm sure isn't the murderer."

"Don't count on it."

They went to Harvey's for stuffed flounder and Phoebe's disposition improved considerably. There was the beginning of a tiff when Henry wouldn't let her order a martini because he didn't think it would go well with Harvey's Salzstangerl, but she forgave him when she tasted these delicious breadsticks with Scotch.

"I have discovered a vacuum chamber big enough for Dr. Kraft," Henry announced, "and it's in the Natural History Building."

"Are you still trying to freeze Dr. Kraft? That's not the way the murderer did it," she said confidently.

"How do you know?"

"The murderer has done each one differently. We're dealing with someone who enjoys his work—"

"Or her work—"

"—Or her work, but it's asking a lot of a woman. We cherish life, we nurture, after all!"

127

"Like Lizzie Borden."

"Killing your parents is different."

Henry tried to picture Phoebe murdering her mother. It didn't seem likely, somehow. "Other than the murderer's supposed penchant for variation, what's wrong with freeze-drying Dr. Kraft and putting him in an exhibit?"

"Unless things have feathers or are covered with hair, I imagine they look rather funny freeze-dried. Like steaks kept too long in the freezer. Or Bill of Rights. Remember how he looked."

Henry shuddered. "He had been cut up. I didn't pay much attention to the fleshtones of his leg."

"Well I did, and you wouldn't have bought it from your butcher looking like that. Even frozen meat has a limited shelf life."

"Shelf life!" Henry's mind cast back two years and more. "I have an idea," he said.

"Tell!" demanded Phoebe and waved her fish knife at him.

"I have to check first with the Atomic Energy Commission, but I think I know how to give Dr. Kraft a longer shelf life."

Henry came to work early. For the first—no, second—time since he came to the Smithsonian, he couldn't wait to get started. The other time had been when it had come to him about Eddie Rickenbacker.

The people out at AEC headquarters in Germantown, Maryland, were by nature early risers, and the man he wished to talk to was always there by eight.

"Hello? Dr. Carson? This is Henry. Henry Scruggs. You remember, I'm with the State Department and I used to be assigned to the Division of International Activities."

"Scruggs? Of course I remember you. Haven't seen you for some time, though."

"It's been close to two years. I'm at the Smithsonian now."

"You are? I thought you said you were with the State Department."

"I am, but I'm on loan again."

"The State Department seems like an unusual employer to let you work all over the place like that."

"I suppose it is. But the reason I called was to find out something about the irradiated meat studies you people did for the Army."

"In what connection?"

"In connection with murder."

"You mean the Smithsonian murders?"

"Yes, I'm surprised you haven't read about me. I found the bodies, or at least three of them."

"I saw the headlines, but I don't read about murder. It disturbs my peace of mind. I need as much of it as I can get, to keep sane out here with these mad bombers." Dr. Carson worked on the so-called peaceful uses of atomic energy, which Henry thought of as "useful pieces."

"Well, if you can stand to think about it for a few minutes as a purely abstract problem, maybe you could tell me if you could extend the shelf life of a human body by irradiating it."

"I suppose you could, though we never tried it, needless to say. The Army will eat most anything, but there are some limits. The thing is, you would have to seal it up. The radiation just sterilizes the meat. You still have to protect it from outside contamination. It works fine on ham and bacon, but I guess you don't plan to smoke your man."

"So there is no way fresh meat can be preserved?"

"I didn't say that. You would just have to enclose the body in a barrier that can withstand biological invasion. You could, I suppose, cover him with Novawood."

"Novawood?"

"Yes. It is a dandy way to preserve wood. It converts it into a plastic in which the cellular structure of the wood just acts as a matrix holding a polymer plastic."

"Explain—"

"You take a piece of wood and put it into a vacuum chamber. You draw a vacuum and then surround the wood with a particular kind of radiation-sensitive gaseous monomer. Release the vac-

uum, and the monomer enters the structure of the wood. Then you subject the wood to gamma radiation and the monomer changes into a polymer plastic. That is an electrochemical bond of molecules.

"It is tough stuff. In theory, you ought to be able to do that to a human body and then sterilize the interior of the flesh for extended shelf life. Eventually, I suppose, it would break down, but for a while it ought to make a pretty good-looking mummy. It should shine up rather nicely, if you can judge by Novawood."

"Dr. Carson, you may just have come up with the answer I need. Thank you very much!"

"If somebody has really preserved a body that way, I would appreciate having the details and, if possible, the body for study. You could send me just an arm, that would be enough. I don't think AEC and the Army would let me process one out here."

Henry was ecstatic. Now to get up to the Spad. He dialed 5866 but there was no answer. Was everybody in the General Counsel's office late for work? He looked at his watch. Eight thirty-five.

Ten minutes crawled by before anybody appeared in FAO and then it was just Mrs. Plumm. That was another point in her favor. "Where is everybody?" he asked her.

"Oh! Mr. Scruggs! You frightened me. There's never anybody here before nine-fifteen."

"Oh. I didn't know. I've never been here this early before. Well, only once. What do you do while you're waiting for everybody?"

"I have my coffee!" She raised a Styrofoam cup for him to see. Coffee, and in plastic. Now there were two points against her. "And I answer the telephone!"

"Does anybody ever call this early?"

"No."

Henry fixed himself some tea and worked on his overseas research survey while he waited for Phoebe to arrive in her office. He called every fifteen minutes. At nine-twenty the OGC receptionist said that she had just come in. Henry looked at his watch and noted the time. Something might have to be done about that if they were to spend the rest of their lives together. She got up far too early. Perhaps today was abnormal. Nobody in their right mind would have expected to see him this early either. Just then Ambassador Craddock looked into his office with mild disbelief.

Finally the receptionist in the General Counsel's office put Henry through to Phoebe. "Hello, Phoebe?"

"Henry! Is that you? Are you calling from home? Are you sick or something?"

"No, I came in early. I had to call a friend at AEC. I figured it out. With a little help from my friend, that is."

"You mean about preserving what's-his-name?" Phoebe was like any other lawyer when it came to distrusting the security of telephones.

"That's exactly what I mean. See you for lunch. I'll tell you all about it. Maybe we should go out somewhere."

"Okay, noon at the east door."

"Eleven-thirty, I can't wait till noon."

At just after ten, Henry had a visit from Inspector Jones, if that is what his name was. "Scruggs? I've got some questions to ask you."

"I'm pretty busy right now." Henry looked busy, but it was mostly because of the mess of papers on his desk.

"Well, I don't mind. I can ask you right here or you can come back with me to the station."

Henry thought that one over for about ten seconds. They would put him in a room again and he would miss his lunch again. And it was lunch with Phoebe! "Sit down and I'll pour you some tea."

Inspector Jones looked suspiciously at Henry's tea but he tasted it a couple of times before forgetting the rest of it while he went down a long checklist of questions.

They were mostly regarding where Henry had been on different days. Apparently, the police had been digging into the movements of the murder victims and had narrowed down the likely times that they were killed. Because of the

131

various means of preservation, forensics had been of little help.

But Henry was impressed that the police had charted the known movements of each victim and had assumed, quite reasonably, that they could not have been alive for very long after the last reported sighting unless they had some reason to keep out of sight. Still, the times were not very specific and the trail was growing cold. It had become increasingly apparent that all the victims had probably been killed at about the same time, and that time had been more than a month ago, probably during the first week of August.

Henry answered the questions as best he could. Inspector Jones just grunted from time to time, leaving Henry quite in the dark whether he was a serious suspect in the crimes.

But Jones departed without putting Henry in handcuffs, so the answers couldn't have been enough to hang him. For the moment.

Hamilton came in the east door while Henry was waiting for Phoebe to come down. She was late and Henry had gone through all the conversation gambits with Mr. Taggart that he could think of, except cars. Henry was asking Mr. Taggart where he should get his car repaired. Henry's car didn't need to be fixed but it was the sort of question that could keep them going until noon if necessary.

Hamilton looked dazed and he looked rumpled. "Henry, dear friend, I have to talk to you!"

Henry could see that Hamilton was far beyond his usual histrionics; in fact, he had never seen him in such a state. He hadn't even addressed him by his diplomatic title, however false. "I'm having lunch with Miss Casey. Perhaps you would like to join us, if you don't mind including her in the discussion."

"No! Not at all! I would love to join both of you. I think I may need a lawyer almost as much as I need your good counsel. Perhaps, if you don't mind, I might give Taylor a ring. He would feel left out if we didn't."

"By all means! I always enjoy mordant company."

Taylor joined them just as Phoebe arrived, unapologetic at keeping Henry waiting twenty minutes. They lunched at the downtown Thai Room amid the splendor of failed Roman excess. It was a cellar that had been given the appearance of a Roman colonial bawdy house by the owners of an earlier restaurant called the Forum of Imperial Rome, which abandoned the premises after a short time. A few weeks of good Thai cooking had served to eradicate all olfactory evidence of the previous owners, but the elaborate plaster and red velvet was taking longer to disappear.

In a dark corner behind the dance floor, they huddled together over larb, spicy bean thread, chicken with hot chili and garlic, and pad Thai. They ordered eight Sing-ha beers to be brought at once so they would not be disturbed. As soon as the waiter brought the food and beer, Hamilton began his story.

"My dears! You have absolutely no idea what I've been through!"

"You've been to see your dentist?" asked Henry, since that was the worst thing he could imagine.

"Worse than that!"

"Your cat is pregnant?" asked Phoebe, in an odd choice of horrors.

"Even than that!"

"The IRS has audited you" was Taylor's guess. He never kept records, as a matter of principle.

"My friends, you see before you the mangled remains of a night in Lubyanka Prison! Note my hollow eyes, my visage transcendent, beyond despair!"

"One night? *Verklaerter* Hamilton?" Henry shook his head. "Nobody spends just one night in Lubyanka. That would be like spending just one night at Acapulco."

"Are you certain it was Lubyanka, Hamilton?" asked Taylor. "It does seem rather far to go for overnight and one prison looks pretty much like another."

"Of course I'm certain! It was right there on Dzerzhinsky Square. Beria himself interrogated me!"

"Did he say his name was Jones?" Henry was beginning to catch on. They had tried the same trick on him.

"He may have. He may have, but I wasn't fooled for a moment!"

"Did he have a Georgian accent?"

"Well, I suppose so, Taylor, but I don't speak anything but Japanese, Swahili, and a bit of Tuareg."

"Just as I thought. You really should learn English, Hamilton. Everybody else speaks it."

"Do be quiet, Taylor. You, too, Henry. Let Hamilton go on with his story. We're listening, Hamilton, at least some of us are. I am."

"Thank you, Phoebe. It was only one night and that must be so because I could not have survived two."

"Begin at the beginning, Hamilton," urged Taylor, "and do try to curb your natural tendency to dramatize the ordinary."

"Well! I am offended! There was nothing ordinary about this!"

"I believe you, Hamilton, dear, or I would believe you if you would ever get around to telling us about it." Phoebe delivered herself of these assurances while helping herself to the last of the bean thread. Henry had not been fast enough. He signaled the waiter for more.

"Thank you, my dear! These men may be our friends, but at the core, they are spiteful and unsympathetic. But the bare and unvarnished facts are these:

"Yesterday afternoon I was sitting at my desk writing a piece for a journal to which I occasionally contribute, when two men from the Cheka—actually one Cheka man and a Cheka woman—burst into my office and dragged me down to their headquarters!"

"Did they take you in a Cheka cab, Hamilton?

"Do shut up, Taylor!"

"Were you handcuffed?" asked Henry. He was unsure of how to work KGB or NKVD into a pun, so he asked something trivial, if to the point.

134

"I might just as well have been. I was marched ahead of these two with pistols clanking on their hips—"

"Do pistols clank?" asked Phoebe.

"I don't honestly know," replied Taylor. "I must pay attention the next time I am arrested."

"I will not be sidetracked from telling my story! I was thrust into a squad car and, with lights flashing and siren shrieking, I was carried off at great danger to myself and to the ordinary citizens on the streets."

"If it was daytime, they weren't ordinary citizens; they were tourists."

"Well, no matter, Taylor, I was in danger! And once they had me in their den, they strip-searched me!"

"I can't believe that," said Phoebe, who grinned with amusement at the thought.

"Well, they emptied out my pockets and patted me down. I think they were homosexuals!"

"The next time I'm arrested," said Henry, "I will certainly call for a policewoman."

Hamilton ignored him. "Then I was shut up in a room, a cell with a single light bulb and a chair."

"It had 256 floor tiles."

"Exactly, Henry. How did you know?"

"I felt your pain last night. Your emotions were so strong that I had a vision. It was so vivid that I woke Phoebe and told her about it."

"That was another one of his visions. I slept alone last night."

"Well, to get back to it, I was held for hours and then they questioned me with rubber truncheons—for hours."

"I don't see any truncheon marks." Taylor had put on his glasses and was looking Hamilton over critically.

"They didn't actually strike me because I told them everything, absolutely everything, they wanted to know. But the threat of the truncheon was always there, and that's just the same."

"Did you admit anything?" Taylor looked uncomfortable.

"I most certainly did!"

135

"You admitted you committed the murders?"

"Of course not! I admitted that I wasn't guilty!"

"You should have admitted otherwise," said Phoebe, putting on her serious lawyer's look. "If you had admitted you murdered everybody, they would have stopped questioning you and we could have gotten you out of jail on bail right away."

"Well, Hamilton," said Taylor, effectively hiding any sympathy he may have felt, "you don't have anything to worry about now. We'll never tell on you."

"That's just the point! Somebody has told the police everything I have said against the eunuchs! How they have abused me!"

"Well, think back," Henry suggested. "To whom have you said these things?"

"Why, to everybody, of course!"

Hamilton had milked last night's ordeal for all it was worth, so he turned to his lunch and Phoebe turned to Henry's discovery. She begged him to tell all.

"I will on two conditions. The first condition is that Hamilton and Taylor agree not to tell anybody anything about it until our investigation is complete, and the second is that they will not interfere."

"What do you mean by interfere?" asked Taylor.

"I mean we don't want you near the Smithsonian after work tomorrow night."

"I don't see how we can possibly agree—"

"What Hamilton is trying to say is that of course we agree." Taylor would say anything to hear a confidence or a rumor.

With some misgivings, Henry recounted his early-morning conversation with Dr. Carson. The second platter of bean thread arrived and more Sing-ha was ordered. Hamilton was most skeptical that Kraft could be preserved in such a way, but Taylor, who knew less about science and more about the variety of man, was convinced Henry was on to something.

Then Henry went on to tell about his visit from Inspector

Jones earlier that morning and how he, Henry, must still be a suspect.

"But they didn't arrest you, dear Henry!" exclaimed Hamilton.

"No, I don't think I'm high on their list."

"Don't count on it. They're just toying with you."

"Giving you rope," added Taylor helpfully. "But get on with you plan, Henry. What is it you are going to do to throw them off the scent?"

"Tomorrow night we'll have to find out whether my theory is correct and I have really located Kraft!" concluded Henry. "It will be the best time because everybody will be gone on Friday evening. That means I will have to buy some rope this afternoon. I'll get two hundred feet to be sure we have enough."

"Rope? What for?" Phoebe looked uneasy.

"So we can climb up to the Spad. It's got to be thirty feet off the floor."

"Who's going to do the climbing? You, Hamilton, or Taylor?"

"Why, Phoebe, you are, of course! I can't stand heights, and our friends have promised to stay out of this."

"Henry, you've lost your mind! In the first place there isn't a chance in a million that Dr. Kraft's body is in that airplane, and in the second place I'm not about to climb up a rope to look."

"You can wear slacks if you're so modest."

"I don't wear slacks. I'm too short. And besides you're a dirty old man to think about that."

"I'm not so old," protested Henry and dug in to his bean thread. It had cooled a bit but was still fiery hot from a pepper point of view. He cooled his mouth off with a swallow of Sing-ha. Delicious.

"My children," said Hamilton, now seeming to be fully recovered from last night's ordeal, "we wouldn't think of letting you undertake this frightful task alone. We will join you. Taylor can do the climbing if it is really dangerous."

They argued through lunch and much of the afternoon,

but Phoebe still refused to climb the rope, and Hamilton and Taylor refused to honor their promise to stay out of the expedition. Against Henry's better judgment, he began to be thankful that the other two were going along and Taylor might do the climbing. It made Henry dizzy to think about it.

 **Eleven**

Thursday, after work (what little work they did that afternoon), Henry and Phoebe went to a hardware store to equip themselves with rope for their investigations. On the way out of the store, Henry saw an archery kit and on impulse bought it. He thought about it for a moment and added some fish line.

Friday seemed endless. Phoebe had to meet with a congressional committee and had lunch on Capitol Hill. Henry looked, without success, for Hamilton and Taylor in the Commons. He might even have welcomed another visit from Inspectors Jones and Smith, somebody to talk to. He was reduced to eating with himself, which, however, did have its points. He could have double chocolate cake for dessert without having anybody make comments about it, and maybe a pretty girl would be unable to find a table and would ask whether she could join him. In which case, he would skip the cake, of course.

He was actually joined by Gerald Blackman. Gerald had been passed over for deputy director of FAO when Ronald Hipster had been hired. This had been just after Henry's arrival. On the surface, Gerald had taken it calmly, but he made no secret that he thought Hipster was an incompetent or worse. "May I join you, Henry?" he asked and sat down before Henry could reply.

Henry got along fine with Gerald as long as they stayed away from politics or religion or related subjects. Henry was an unashamed liberal and Gerald was quite conservative. Henry could not take organized religion seriously and Gerald took it literally. After the first few months of heated debate, they had learned to enjoy each other's company in harmless fields such as music, art, and even office gossip. Among the few things they agreed upon perfectly were sports and opera. Neither gave a damn about them. Oh, yes, and Ronald Hipster.

"What did you think of Mr. Hipster's actions on Tuesday?" Gerald asked, as though moving pawn to king four.

"I'm afraid he's gone completely insane. He's just lucky that doesn't disqualify him from working at the Smithsonian."

"He hasn't come in since then."

"I assumed that, though I was out with visitors most of Wednesday, myself." Henry looked at his watch. "There's still a chance he might come in today."

"I doubt it. He's been spending most of his afternoons in a topless bar."

"I wonder if he'd like company?" Henry asked. Actually, he was wondering how Gerald had learned about the bar. He was a little surprised Gerald knew they existed, though now that he thought about it, he decided that topless bars were probably preached against in church. Henry would have to visit church sometime and find out if there were any sins he had overlooked.

"Have you found Dr. Kraft's body yet?" Gerald asked, quickly changing the subject from sex, which he was uncomfortable talking about, to murder, which didn't bother him a bit.

"I think so. I just have to test an hypothesis."

"Well, I hope you can find him so you can get back to your overseas research survey. The Secretary's been asking for it and Craddock is about to put me on it to get it done."

140

"If you'd like to help out, by all means do, but I expect to be able to resume work on the survey next week. I should have everybody in jail by then."

Then they put business aside for more important things. Gerald liked cake, too.

Ordinarily, Fridays during the best times of the year are short. Everybody tries to get away early and after about three-thirty it is hard to find anybody in the Castle. This Friday crawled. Not so much because people stayed around later than usual but because Henry was eager to get started on the evening's adventure.

Henry and Gerald ate their chocolate cake with full attention. Neither wished to spoil his concentration on the taste by talking. In truth, however, Henry's attention wandered from the cake. He sat, eating silently, and willing people to go home early. Have a migraine. Go watch your kids play softball. Just go do something as long as you go. It didn't do any good. People lingered over coffee. They stood outside watching nubile tourist girls (or boys) before going back up to their offices. They fiddled around, wasting time. Henry's time.

After Henry and Gerald climbed back to the FAO offices, Henry lagging behind to get a careful count (it would not do, today, to get it wrong). Henry went over to the wall clock and thumped it with the flat of his hand to make it go faster. It seemed to work; the minute hand moved a couple of steps. Five o'clock and Phoebe eventually came together at the head of the steps. Thirty minutes later, after the museums closed and the area was suddenly almost deserted, they descended from the tower and retrieved their equipment from the trunk of Henry's car.

They had chosen nylon rope because it was stronger without being bulky. Still, two hundred feet of it was hard to hide. And there was no way to conceal the bow. So Henry walked past the guard with the spool of fish line stuck on a finger and proceeded to his office. Counting as usual. He already knew how many steps there were—they had been holding at sixty-two for days, now—but it established a

141

rhythm, he decided, that helped him to collect his thoughts.

From his office window in the tower, Henry dropped the end of the fish line weighted with a glue bottle. Phoebe tied the end of the rope onto the fish line and he hauled it up as a few remaining tourists looked on curiously. The rope was followed by the bow and a bundle of arrows. "We are putting on a pageant," Phoebe told her audience, "cowboys and Indians."

Phoebe caught up with Taylor and Hamilton climbing back to the tower. They had an hour to kill before the guard force would be finished with their supper and settled down for the night. Henry unlocked his classified files cabinet and pulled out a bottle of Talisker. He poured out glasses of the whisky for all.

"Somebody ought to stay sober," suggested Phoebe.

"You may if you wish, but I don't recommend it." Taylor held out his glass for a refill.

Henry sipped his drink slowly, hoping to find that narrow walkway between courage and inebriation. Once he found it, he made another pot of tea to keep from going over the edge. Meanwhile, Hamilton and Taylor plunged happily over the brink and into cheerful drunkenness. It was hard to tell about Phoebe. Phoebe drunk was a lot like Phoebe sober. Or perhaps Phoebe sober was a lot like Phoebe drunk.

With summer over, the Smithsonian was pretty well cleared out by seven o'clock. It was time the conspirators got under way. Earlier in the day, Phoebe had placed a bit of glass fiber tape on the door catch leading to the back way into Public Affairs. Now, they had only to descend one flight of steps (a long one, twenty-six steps) down to the second floor, where they could trip the lock on the Public Affairs door and cross through those offices and out the Public Affairs front door to reach the west balcony. This avoided the main floor entirely and considerably reduced the chances of encountering a stray guard.

After museum closing, the light in the galleries was greatly reduced, to something a little better than the light of a full moon. It seemed dark at first, but after the eyes adjusted to it, it was quite bright. The Spads were startling. One was upside down, at the top of an evasive loop that took it up against the roof trusses high over the make-believe airstrip. The other Spad banked at a little above balcony height to bring its guns to bear upon some unseen craft from Richthofen's *Jagdgeschwader,* the Red Baron's *Flying Circus.*

It was that aggressive aerial warrior in the attacking Spad that Henry knew had to be Dr. Kraft. Henry risked shining his flashlight on the body in the plane, twenty-five feet away. Under the helmet and goggles and above the trailing white scarf a face showed an evil grin that meant Henry had to be right.

"I thought we could rig it from up here," Henry whispered to Taylor, "and then you could go down to climb up from below. But this nylon rope is so smooth I'm afraid you can't grip it to climb it."

"Why don't you swing over from the balcony?"

"Me? Because I would swing right into the side of plane. No thanks. Besides, you're going to do it."

"I suffer from vertigo," announced Taylor.

"Why didn't you say so?" Henry was becoming exasperated.

"Nobody asked me. I get into a cold sweat when I get near the edge of the balcony."

"I could play out the rope and let you swing over slowly," said Phoebe.

"You're not strong enough. Or heavy enough. If we are going to do it that way, Hamilton will have to handle the rope."

Hamilton looked doubtful. "I'm afraid I'm not the athletic type, Henry. I could wrap the rope a couple of turns around the rail. That way I could get you over. But I don't think I could get you back."

"Thanks, but I don't want to become a permanent part of the exhibit."

"You men simply aren't practical; you do everything the

hard way. You wouldn't have to come back. You could descend to the floor."

"I'll worry about that when I figure out how to get the rope over the truss above the Spad."

"I thought that was what you brought the bow and arrows for," said Phoebe.

"Yeah, but I've got to get the fish line through the right part of the truss and then catch the line on the other side and bring it back to here so we can pull the rope through. I'm not very good at this."

"Give it here!" Phoebe tied the fish line onto an arrow and then laid almost a hundred feet of the line out on the floor in a long zigzag. Then she shot the arrow through the truss. It disappeared into the gloom on the other side of the gallery. "Go get it," she ordered.

Henry did as he was told, not expecting to find anything, and walked along the U-shaped balcony that enclosed three sides of the gallery. He didn't find it; it found him. His face ran into the fish line at the far end of the opposite balcony. The arrow was stuck in a door. Henry retrieved the end of the line and returned to Phoebe. "How did you learn to do that?"

"Summer camp. If your parents are divorced, you spend a lot of time in summer camp."

They stretched the rope out along the balcony, pushing useless Hamilton and Taylor out of the way, and Phoebe tied a series of bowline knots, making a sort of ladder with a single line and a series of loops. "Girl Scouts," she explained. "If your parents are—" Henry had spent a lot of time in the Boy Scouts, but he never learned the bowline. Of course his parents weren't divorced. Then the rope ladder was pulled through the truss with the fish line, the end barely making it across the truss without the fish line breaking. Once the ladder was in place and pulled back to the balcony, another piece of the rope, knotted at intervals, was attached to the lower end of the ladder. Phoebe would use that to control Henry's swing across to the plane.

144

Henry had brought his bottle and took a last swig before sailing off into the night to do battle high over an advance airfield in France. Taylor and Hamilton solemnly shook his hand and Phoebe embraced him with tears flowing down her cheeks. She gave him a handkerchief to tie around his neck.

His departure from the balcony was sickening until he came to expect the jerks as the guide rope played out over the balcony rail. Henry dealt with the distance to the floor by looking up to the roof. It was equally bad. He settled on staring fixedly at the Spad and the plastic grin of Dr. Kraft. The rope ladder brought him right against the place where the trailing edge of the lower wing joins the fuselage, but about twenty inches too low. He cautiously inserted his free foot into a higher loop and raised himself. He still couldn't quite see into the cockpit.

He extracted his lower foot from its loop and placed it on the wing of the Spad. The Spad abruptly heeled over another twenty degrees and the rigging that held it groaned loudly. Henry was swung out into space and as the Spad resumed its normal position, he found himself swinging back, pendulum-like, on a collision course with the Spad. Phoebe and Hamilton pulled back the slack on the guide rope and braced themselves to catch Henry. He stopped with a jerk six inches from the plane.

He heard footsteps below and looked down. A guard had come into the exhibit, attracted by the noise. Henry knew he was going to look up.

The guard did indeed look up, and he saw the stunting Spads. He had never paid any attention to them before. There was a figure suspended from a rope ladder, one arm and one leg outstretched. The ladder was obviously supposed to be from the higher airplane, but anybody could tell the rope was wrong. You could see where it was attached to the roof truss. Even in this light. The exhibits people shouldn't have used such a white rope. Well, nobody's here and it's time for the second half of the seventh inning. He walked out of the hall and Henry breathed again.

Henry resumed a pose more in keeping with his feelings—terror—and inched his way up the rope ladder. His head rose level with the pilot of the Spad. Wrapping the rope around his left arm, Henry fished in a pocket for his flashlight. He turned it on and looked in the face of death. It looked more contorted and evil from this close view.

"Is that him?" came Phoebe's stage whisper from the balcony.

"He," said Henry.

"It is!?"

"No, I mean you should ask 'Is that he?' It is a predicate nominative."

"Fuck you, Henry!"

Henry was shocked. He hadn't known Phoebe used words such as that. Hamilton was openmouthed, and Taylor amused.

"I don't know yet. He looks sort of funny and plastic." Henry transferred the flashlight to his left hand, the one wound up with the rope, and hunted in his hip pocket for his pocket knife. It was going to take two hands to open it, so he had to move the flashlight again. This time he tucked it into the jacket of the flyer. The upward beam of light transformed the face into a devil's visage. Henry shuddered and concentrated on opening the knife.

Henry thought again about how much he disliked Kraft and jabbed at his face with his knife. It barely scratched it. "It seems like plastic," he whispered.

"Isn't that what you thought it would be like?"

"Yes, but I thought if would feel different." He took the handle of his knife and tapped the pilot's nose. "It sounds hollow," he whispered. Henry folded up his knife and put it in his pocket, then he raised himself another rung. Retrieving his flashlight he turned it down toward the pilot's lower body. There wasn't any.

"Let the guide rope fall, Phoebe, I'm going to climb down. This is only a dummy!"

* * *

After his descent, Henry climbed up the stairs at the end of the balcony and helped Phoebe retrieve the rope. "I'm sure Kraft can't be in the other Spad. It would be too much for one person to put the body in an upside-down airplane. But leave the knots in the rope for the moment. We ought to check Mr. Wright while we're at it."

"He's dead, remember? His was the cut-and-dried case."

"Not your Mr. Wright, but one of the other ones. In the Wright Flyer. That dummy wears a cap and goggles. It's just possible—"

"Miss Casey is always looking for Mister Right," said Taylor, predictably, "all girls are."

Phoebe extended her middle finger at him, shocking Henry once again.

They set up the same rig to get to the Wright Flyer. The Flyer was lower than the Spad and in better light. However, it presented two additional problems. The guard room was just the other side of the inner front doors, and the pilot of the Flyer sat so far back that someone was going to have to board the aircraft to check on the dummy.

"You men are going to be too heavy. And besides, Henry's really clumsy. I'll have to go."

"I won't try to talk you out of it, but remember you'll have to support yourself on the structural parts of the Flyer. I'm almost sure the covering has been replaced but it wasn't designed to walk on."

"I'll be careful, Henry."

"And Phoebe, sweetheart—"

"Yes, dear?" Phoebe's voice betrayed a bit of sarcasm at Henry's uncharacteristically intimate talk.

"You won't break it, will you? I can't think of anything in the Smithsonian I would less want to damage."

Phoebe proved to be quite agile, something else she learned in summer camp or perhaps dodging fighting parents, Henry supposed. She removed Mr. Wright's hat and goggles and even from the balcony Henry could tell it was Dr. Kraft.

"He's beginning to stink, Henry. I don't think this was a

very good way to preserve a body," said Phoebe rather calmly, all things considered.

"Put up your hands, and don't move, not even a little bit!" The lights in the north range came on with blinding suddenness.

 *Twelve*

Phoebe refused to come down from the Wright Flyer while the guard stood below. She wouldn't explain, but she used both hands to hold her skimpy leather skirt close to her thighs. She was still sitting there, on the wing of the plane, when the Park Service Police arrived.

"Come down from there, Miss!" said Park Police Inspector Floyd Haselton sternly.

"Stay right where you are, honey," said Park Police Corporal Alice Varner. "I'll make these men move out of the way." Corporal Varner caught one of the Smithsonian guards by the arm and started to drag him from below the Flyer.

There was a sudden sound of fabric ripping and Phoebe abruptly began to descend, accelerating at thirty-two feet per second. A startled Inspector Haselton put out his arms and caught her. It was reflexive; he didn't have time to think about it or he might have let her fall, seeing that she was apprehended *in flagrante delicto,* doing what, he wasn't quite sure.

Henry didn't see what had happened because at the first sound of tearing fabric, he had closed his eyes, his worst fears being realized, worse than the dentist, even worse than a pregnant cat.

Henry and Hamilton were brought down from the balcony in handcuffs. They were then cuffed to Phoebe. "You are all three under arrest," announced Inspector Haselton.

"I rather gathered that," said Henry, looking around to see where Taylor had got to. "I want my lawyer."

"You can call him from headquarters."

"She's right here."

"Yes, you've got to read them—us—our rights."

"Goddamn! This is a first! You two guys going on a job with your lawyer!"

"Read—"

"Oh, okay. *Okay!* You are under arrest. You have the right to remain silent. Anything you say may be taken down in evidence and used against you. Both, uh, all three of you. You have the right to an attorney—"

"You can skip that part. There's a body up there," said Phoebe.

"I don't see no body," said the duty sergeant of the Smithsonian guard force. "Only the dummy that's always been there."

"Corporal, better telephone ahead and have them get ready for drug testing. Tell them it's LSD or something like it."

There was the sound of a door bursting open behind some exhibits cases and McKeown came striding in. "What the hell's going on?" he demanded.

"Sir," said the duty sergeant, "we caught these three trying to destroy the Flyer, sir."

"What's the Park Police doing here? They're not supposed to be here! This is Smithsonian jurisdiction!"

"I thought that was only in the Castle, sir. I called them," the sergeant said uncomfortably.

"No, I think—" McKeown looked behind the Park Police at the prisoners for the first time. "Scruggs? Casey? Sealyham? Are you the ones they caught?"

Phoebe spoke up. "It's us."

"We," said Henry. Hamilton said nothing, but looked mournful at the thought of going back to Lubyanka so soon.

150

"Shut up, Henry, it's all three of us."

"That's okay, then. The dative lives happily with the accusative," Henry whispered in her ear and then closed his mouth down over it.

Phoebe jerked as far away as she could, what with being handcuffed to Henry, and returned to business. "The Park Police have jurisdiction in the A and I. We've got it in the Castle. But you might want to get somebody to look up in the Wright Flyer. That's Dr. Kraft."

The Park Police looked skeptical when McKeown explained that Phoebe was the Smithsonian's Assistant General Counsel, but after McKeown got the guards to find ladders and climb up to the Flyer, and after the body of Dr. Kraft was identified, the Park Police were considerably happier. They now had a piece of the action.

The Washington Metropolitan Police had been called in for the other murders, on the grounds that the murders had probably occurred in the Castle, and the Smithsonian jurisdiction fell short of murder. There had been some argument about that, but the Under Secretary had ordered McKeown to call the police, so that was that.

As the publicity over the murders waxed with each discovered body, the Washington police were widely interviewed and quoted, and the Park Police had begun to feel left out. Neglected and more than a bit jealous.

Now they had their own body and they would be able to play it for all it was worth. And before Congress! It would miss this budget cycle but it would catch the next. Important new duties! Investigating the serial murders at the Smithsonian! Apprehending the dangerous madman! It ought to be good for another ten million in the budget, minimum!

Eventually, Henry and Hamilton were released in the custody of their lawyer. "Where do you suppose Taylor went?" Phoebe asked nobody in particular.

"I think he hid in the security offices on the balcony. They always leave them unlocked and nobody would ever think of

151

looking there. He's probably gone from Washington by now. Phoebe, I think we should do the same. I expect that both the metropolitan Police and the National Capital Park Police are going to want to talk to us some more and I'm sure the press will. It will ruin our weekend if we don't go someplace."

"The Park Police said not to."

"What could they do?"

"We could be arrested as material witnesses."

"They would have to find us. We could go somewhere in Maryland or Virginia where they don't have jurisdiction. They would have to ask the state police to go look for us. That would take days. And even if they found us, we don't have any information regarding the murderer. They couldn't hold us."

"No, I suppose not."

"Well, I'm willing to leave town." Hamilton was still sweating from his second questioning by the police. "I certainly don't want to be around when those KGB people come after me again. And besides, you two will have to have a chaperone."

"We are going to take you home to your wife, if she wants you back," Phoebe said. "Henry and I are the ones who are leaving town and you don't have to worry about my virtue. Lawyers don't have any. Where do you live?"

"I'm not going to tell." Hamilton was beginning to pout.

"I know where he lives. It's in Alexandria."

They loaded into Henry's car and turned left from Independence Avenue at Fourteenth Street (an illegal turn) and headed for the Rochambeau Bridge into Virginia.

Henry felt positively revived when he returned on Wednesday. It had been quite an excursion and had rained the whole time, washing out Henry's hay fever entirely. He felt wonderful!

They had driven southeast along the Potomac without seeing any place they wanted to stop, and when they came to the Route 301 bridge, they crossed north into Maryland, turned toward Annapolis, crossed the Chesapeake Bay onto the Eastern Shore, and eventually found themselves in St. Michaels. The inn there was closed up for the night, but they slept in the car and checked in at breakfast time.

They had considered going back on Monday, but they hadn't caught up on their sleep yet. Or whatever. On Tuesday, Phoebe had called her office over Henry's protest, and even across the room, Henry could hear Associate General Counsel Habeas Corpus yelling at Phoebe. She replied, "Okay! Okay! Mr. Bodde, we'll come back tomorrow!"

Back in Washington, Henry bounced up the stairs (54, the landing, 56, 58, 60, 62) to his tower office. Craddock heard him coming and called from his office before Henry made it back to his desk. "Scruggs! Get in here!" Not "Will you please" or even just "Come in" but "Get in"!

"Yes, sir!" Henry sat down without being asked. "It's nice to be back," he said gratuitously and somewhat inanely.

"Where in the Goddamn hell have you been?"

Such language from a former ambassador! "I had to get away to think. And to avoid the press. You said before that I talked too much to the press."

"The Under Secretary is fit to be tied!"

"I don't see why. Miss Casey and I found the missing body for him. Surely somebody else can find out who did it."

"Do you know?"

"Why should I know?" Henry was now being coy, one of his annoying traits.

"You seem to know everything else about this business."

"Well, I think I know who the murderer is, but I don't have any evidence."

"Who is it, then?"

"I couldn't say without some proof."

"Get the hell over to the Under Secretary's office!"

The Under Secretary had called in McKeown between the time Henry telephoned and his arrival on the second floor of the Castle. There was a short replay of demanding to know where Henry had been, but there was such general

153

approval of Henry's staying away from the press that any criticism was quickly dropped.

"We are waiting for Miss Casey, but you might be interested to know that the autopsy reveals that Dr. Kraft was stabbed. Apparently something like a letter opener was thrust through him from behind. It pierced his heart and he must have died almost immediately. You might begin by explaining how you knew where to find Dr. Kraft."

"I just tried to think like the murderer. It was the last of all the different ways I could think of to hide a body."

"And what the hell was done to the body? It looks like somebody tried to preserve it but the medical examiner can't figure out what they did to it."

"They made it into Novabody."

"What on earth is that?"

"It's a new process. The murderer invented it. I wouldn't buy stock in it if I were you; I don't think it works very well." Henry forestalled the Under Secretary's apoplexy by explaining the process. "I think the murderer is running out of ideas for preserving bodies."

"And just why do you think the murderer is so determined to preserve his victims?"

Phoebe came in quietly and sat down. Henry smiled at her in a doting way and turned back to the Under Secretary.

"I think it is all a matter of time. You can't come in or out of the Smithsonian buildings after hours without signing the guard's register. If you know when a crime is committed, you can limit the number of suspects by checking to see who is on the premises at the time. With four murders there would probably be only one suspect who was in the proper building each time a murder was committed. But if you make it impossible to tell when the crime is committed, you make all of the staff into suspects."

"I suppose that makes a certain amount of sense, unless the crime is committed during business hours when people don't sign in and out."

"That is always possible, but our four murders all required quite a bit of moving bodies around. It is hard to believe this was done in full view of the staff and the daily herd of visitors."

"Besides," said Phoebe, "we think we know who did it."

"Maybe we know. But maybe the person we are thinking about is herself a potential victim."

"She's the murderess. I don't like her."

"You had better explain yourselves," said McKeown.

"Okay, but I want you to know," said Henry, "that this is something less than an accusation. Some investigation will have to be done first."

"It won't leave this room until we have some sort of proof," said the Under Secretary.

"You think she's guilty, Phoebe, do you want to explain?"

"I'd be happy to. All the victims are members of the committee to study the IPES. Only one committee member has survived, and that's Dr. Haas. As Exchange Librarian, she is the only one who regularly uses IPES services. There has to be something going on at IPES that she can't afford to have known. Therefore, she has murdered them all to keep them quiet."

"Isn't that a little drastic?" asked the Under Secretary. "What could drive somebody to the risk of multiple murders? Killing people would seem to be a far greater danger than anything that could be done at IPES."

"Greed," Henry said. "That's what makes people do things like that unless they are crazy. Both may apply here. But it is always possible that someone else is the murderer and Dr. Haas may become a victim when the murderer works out the necessary means.

"Insofar as opportunity is concerned, I like Dr. Haas as a murderess. There are branch libraries in almost every building. The library is always sending cartons of books from building to building. It would be simple enough for a clever librarian to have something taken to the A and I Building by the labor force. Boxes of books are heavy and nobody looks inside. Boxes of books are always just sitting around being ignored unless they are in the way."

"Let's go talk to Dr. Haas," suggested McKeown.

"Are you going to go up to her and accuse her?" asked Phoebe.

"I don't know yet." They had given McKeown a lot to think about. All those books going to and fro. He would have to come up with a procedure. That was always the answer in matters of security.

McKeown, Phoebe, and Henry trooped over to the Natural History Building to the Exchange Librarian's office. There were lots of nearsighted people moving quietly around, but no Dr. Haas.

Nobody had seen Dr. Haas since Monday afternoon. "She may have come in after hours," said her secretary, "because we've gotten a lot of packages sent to her attention and when I came in this morning, some of them appeared to have been moved about and opened. Nobody ever touches her stuff. She's very strict about that."

Henry looked at the packages. Most had not been opened and were neatly stacked wherever a place could be found. These had come from libraries in the United States or abroad, but none appeared to have come through IPES. A few packages were carelessly strewn around with their wrappings ripped open. Henry checked their wrappers. All had been addressed to Dr. Haas in care of IPES. It was obvious that they had been sent over to her unopened.

"Col. McKeown, I think we ought to go out to Anacostia and have a look at IPES," Henry said, stating the obvious.

During the drive in a guard force car, Henry sat in the backseat with Phoebe and thought. What is another way to dispose of a body, assuming there was another one they hadn't found? "I just don't know," he said to Phoebe.

"There are undoubtedly lots of things you don't know, Henry. What, particularly, do you have in mind? Or perhaps I should say, don't you have in mind?"

Henry scowled at Phoebe. He didn't like it when Phoebe did it to him. "I don't want to believe that the murderer repeated himself when he disposed of Dr. Haas."

"Now you call the murderer a he."

"I think so. It is likely that she may have been eliminated, and she was our only female suspect."

"Well, maybe he ate her, whoever he is."

"Ate her! That's it!" Henry gripped Phoebe's arm.

"Henry, you've flipped! I didn't really mean—"

"The murderer didn't eat her," Henry said, "but he found someone who did!" McKeown looked around from the front seat, trying to tune in on their conversation. "I'll explain when we get back."

The IPES chief clerk, Mr. Teddie, was not expecting them. He and one of his assistants had just broken open a large ocean shipment from the National Exchange Library in Ulan Bator and was sorting small packages and envelopes into lots for forwarding to libraries all across the United States. They were preparing to put U.S. postage on the individual packages and where there were a number of pieces going to a single place, to put them into U.S. mailbags. As usual, Mr. Teddie was working dressed in a white shirt and a tie. Loud gospel music was blaring out of a radio that owed nothing to high fidelity.

"Good afternoon, sir," he yelled politely when he saw Henry. "Oh, hello Col. McKeown," and he nodded to Phoebe and added, "ma'am." He was beginning to look rather uncomfortable because he couldn't decide why the head of security was there. Mr. Teddie wouldn't have dreamed of doing anything illegal, but, being black, he knew that if the police chose to look for something improper, they would generally find it.

"Mr. Teddie, this is Miss Casey, the Assistant General Counsel." Now Mr. Teddie showed signs of panic. The law and now a lawyer. That probably meant big trouble.

"Do you suppose," Henry shouted, "we might turn down the radio?"

"Yes, sir!" Mr. Teddie motioned to his assistant who hurried to turn off the gospel music that had been filling the premises with sound.

The relief was immediate. "Thank you, that is much better. Now, Mr. Teddie, we are looking into the IPES traffic

157

that goes to and from the exchange librarian, Dr. Haas. I gather there's a lot of it?"

"Yes, sir! Quite a bit of it. It has increased I'd say two, three times since Dr. Haas arrived." Mr. Teddie was being cooperative. That was always the thing to do.

"Have you sent over anything recently?" asked McKeown.

"Monday. Johnny, wasn't it Monday?" Johnny nodded in assent. Johnny was standing well away from Mr. Teddie so he could disassociate himself from him if necessary. He liked Mr. Teddie, but there were limits on how far you could go for somebody.

"When do you think you will have anything else for her?"

"Nothing here except a couple of envelopes." Mr. Teddie indicated the contents of the Ulan Bator shipment. "But there's probably lots of stuff in the shipments out of South America." He was getting comfortable and professional again. It was Dr. Haas they were after and she could take care of herself, she sure could.

"When do they come in?"

"They are right over there." He pointed to several large shipping pallets piled high with cartons."

"When will you get them open?"

"Maybe Monday. I have a big shipment from the National Diet Library in Japan that's ahead of the South American stuff."

"Do you think," McKeown asked, "you could get to them now? It's important."

"Well, sir, if I was to open them now and get them mixed up with what I already have on the tables, I would mess up my records. I expect we could get the tables clear this afternoon and open one tomorrow, if necessary."

"It's necessary."

"The way I see it, either Dr. Haas has skipped out or someone has added her to the list of Smithsonian murders," said Henry on the way back to town.

"But you don't know which and you don't even know why," said the Colonel.

158

"Correct. But with any kind of luck, tomorrow we will know why, and I have an idea how to find out whether she's been murdered. Miss Casey put me on to it on the trip out."

"All I said was that maybe the murderer ate her."

"Exactly! The murderer caused her to be eaten! And who eats people?"

"Lions," said Phoebe softly, her eyes shining. She grabbed Henry and pulled him over on her and they dissolved in laughter. "Don't go in the lions' cage tonight, mother dear, the lions are ferocious and may bite!" they chorused. They laughed until tears ran down their cheeks.

"You two have really gone nuts," said Col. McKeown with certainty. "I suppose it comes from finding so many stiffs."

Henry controlled himself with difficulty. "No sir, Colonel, we have just learned to think like the murderer. I think if you check the lion cages at the zoo, or maybe the tiger cages, it could be either, you will find some of the remains of Dr. Haas. You'll have to hurry. I imagine the cats will eventually eat bones and all and they've probably been at it since yesterday."

While McKeown may not have actually believed them, his experiences since the first murder was discovered had conditioned him to check out any and all of Henry and Phoebe's crack-brained ideas.

At Henry's suggestion, they picked up dignified old Dr. Mayes and took him out to the zoo. Dr. Mayes borrowed some rubber gloves and an apron from the zoo's hospital, and after the keepers had run the lions back into holding cages, he set about to examine their dinner. It was a messy business but it didn't seem to bother Dr. Mayes very much. Phoebe watched intently and Henry wandered off to look at the monkeys. He decided he didn't really like carnivores.

"Yes," said Dr. Mayes happily when he was finished, "definitely human, at least some of it. I've taken some tissue samples so we can do blood analysis to be certain, but I don't think I could be wrong. There's enough bone left to be sure the kitties aren't getting horse meat or anything like that.

I've told the keepers to gather it all up and put it on ice so the coroner will have something left to look at."

The director of the zoo had arrived while Dr. Mayes was in the cages. He was beginning to feel that he had cause to be unhappy. "Perhaps it might be better just to let the cats eat up what's left. It won't matter to whomever it was, and it might avoid any bad publicity. Schoolchildren don't like animals that eat people."

"They've all been brainwashed by Walt Disney," Henry observed, having returned from the apes.

"You can't possibly suggest we leave the remains of the body to the lions!" said McKeown. "That would be abetting a felony."

"No, I suppose not, but from the zookeeper's perspective it would be a better thing to do. The lions would simply regard it as lunch."

Lunch was a word that hit home to Henry. It was now a few minutes after three and he had not yet had any. But the Under Secretary was waiting and it seemed probable that Henry's lunch would be indefinitely delayed.

"Scruggs, you and Miss Casey seem to have done it again. In view of the nature of this affair, I can't find it in my heart to congratulate you. Dr. Mayes, I suppose there is no real possibility that you might be wrong?"

"No, not really. There were certain joints that were really quite distinctively human. Of course all the major bones had been sawn into rather small pieces, but as I explained to these gentlemen, tissue and blood analysis will make it conclusive. We can even tell the blood type and, I think, sex, but a positive identification of the individual would require finding the head."

"You're sure the head was not among the, uh, remains?"

"Oh, I think it highly unlikely. You see, the keepers fed the body to the lions. Cut up as it was, it almost certainly would have looked rather like the lions' usual diet, but a human head would be quite distinctive. I rather think the head has been disposed of in some other fashion."

"You realize," said Henry, "that this certainly means we still have a murderer on the loose, and we have no idea who he is. In a sense, I'm relieved. I wouldn't like to think of a doctor of library science going around murdering people."

"But Dr. Haas was not trained as a librarian, although she was very good at it," said the Under Secretary. "She was an invertebrate zoologist. A gastropodist, to be precise, like the Secretary."

Thirteen

The newspapers caught up with Henry on Thursday morning. All three of the city's principal dailies and United Press International converged on Henry's small row house during breakfast and forced him to hold an impromptu press conference.

"Yes?"

"Mr. Scruggs? May we come in?" Four reporters and three photographers pushed past Henry into his living room and followed Henry as he retreated into the dining room where Phoebe was applying fig preserves to toast.

"What the hell do you want?" Henry was outraged at having his morning tea interrupted. Phoebe posed in dishabille (almost) for the three photographers who dazzled Henry's eyes with their strobe lights.

DAILY NEWS: "We want to talk about the Smith-sonian's horrible daemon murderer."

UPI: "Is this Mrs. Scruggs?"

HENRY: "Well, yes. Actually, this is my mother. She's just come up here from Tennessee.

POST: "She doesn't look old enough to be your mother, in fact she looks younger than you are."

HENRY: "Girls get married very young in Tennessee. She was only a child."

STAR: "Is it true that you and a Miss Casey have discovered five bodies in the Smithsonian."

HENRY: "So far."

DAILY NEWS: "You mean there are more?"

HENRY: "We have no reason to believe that we have discovered all of them. That's all I can say about that."

UPI: "How do you account for being able to find the bodies when nobody else can?"

HENRY: "Anybody can find them once we tell them where they are."

POST: "We have heard it said that you are the murderer. Is there any truth in that?"

HENRY: "Do you mean 'you' to include both Miss Casey and myself?"

POST: "You can take it any way you like."

HENRY: "Well, I have to know, because my answer depends on it."

DAILY NEWS: May we take that to mean that one of you is the murderer?"

PHOEBE: "Henry, I don't think we should answer that."

STAR: "What has your mother got to do with this?"

HENRY: "She is acting in her capacity as my attorney. Thank you, Mother."

POST: "If I write that you admit you are a mass murderer, could my editors call and clear my copy with you?"

HENRY: "Certainly. My office phone number is 381-5091. I suppose you ought to clear it with the Office of General Counsel as well."

UPI: "Is that the Smithsonian General Counsel?"

HENRY: "Yes. Actually the General Counsel is one of the murder victims. But you can talk to Miss Casey. She is the Assistant General Counsel."

STAR: "And her number is?"

PHOEBE: "The number is 381-5866."

DAILY NEWS: Why does your mother know the General Counsel's number?"

HENRY: "She and Miss Casey were in law school together."

POST: "What about the murder at the National Zoo? Is it true that the lions ate a person up?"

HENRY: "We don't know that for certain."

POST: "Do you mean that no body has been found? The police report seems to indicate otherwise."

HENRY: "No, I mean that we do not know that it was only one body. We won't know that until the laboratory work is complete."

DAILY NEWS: Why do you think that there might be more than one? Did you have a blackout?"

STAR: "He means amnesia. Do you remember what you did that night?"

HENRY: "Which night is that?"

DAILY NEWS: "The night of the murder."

HENRY: "Oh. No, I don't. But as I was saying, the body, if it was only one, was cut up in rather small pieces. I imagine the lions would have just as soon had it whole. They like to put their paws on their supper when they chew it."

UPI (looking rather nauseous): "Is there anything else we should know about the murder at the Zoo?"

HENRY: "Only the head."

DAILY NEWS and UPI together: "The head? What about the head?"

HENRY: "Only that it is missing. It is probably around the Smithsonian someplace."

Henry and Phoebe finally extracted themselves from the press. Henry gave them the idea to leave by sharpening his French butcher knife. He kept it very keen because on Sunday mornings he made an odd but delicious breakfast (so some think, but others disagree) in which two-week-old seedless rye from Posin's bakery is sliced very thin (about a sixteenth of an inch), then soaked in beaten egg and cinnamon, and finally placed on a buttered pizza pan and cooked

164

in a 500-degree oven for 90 seconds. It is then eaten with apricot marmalade or fig preserves, if you have them available. Anyway, the knife could be seen to be very sharp and it made the visitors rather uncomfortable.

It was obvious from the first that little of the real work of the Smithsonian was going to get done that day. News of something nasty in the lions' cage had spread throughout the Smithsonian like salmonella at a summer camp. Before leaving his house, Henry called McKeown's office and learned that the colonel had already left for IPES, so he and Phoebe decided to go directly to Anacostia.

Mr. Teddie had the long sorting tables cleared off and was just breaking open the first of the South American shipping cases. Then he and Johnny set to sorting the contents and laying out the envelopes and packages according to the arcane patterns that had been established at IPES over the previous 120 years. It was tedious and in fact maddening for those investigating the murders.

Eventually, a small group of packages began accumulating in the spot ordained for the Smithsonian Libraries Exchange Librarian. Next to it a much larger pile was a-building for the Smithsonian Libraries, but not addressed to the Exchange Librarian.

"Do you always keep these separate?" Henry asked.

"Oh, yes! Miz Haas would pitch a fit if we were to mix them up. We always have to do it this way."

"I'm afraid we're going to have to open some of Dr. Haas's packages, Mr. Teddie."

"I don't think I can allow you to do that! That's against my instructions."

"It's all right, I'll authorize it, Mr. Teddie," said McKeown.

"Well, if you say so, Colonel, but I'll have to have your written order."

Everything came to a stop while Henry typed out the necessary memorandum on an obsolete Underwood typewriter dating from the days when IPES was a major operation. Phoebe was a faster and better typist (women have such clever fingers), but she refused to do it on principle and resented being asked. [Let the record show that Henry was not the one who suggested it.] And of course Phoebe was too young to have ever used a manual typewriter and didn't know how to make the carriage go back.

The first five packages they opened were publications on this and that, including experiments on trace metals in cattle feeding and notes on sea-horse mating rituals. Package number six was a reasonably large book in Spanish on crop rotation in upland rain forests. When the book was opened it proved to be mostly a large plastic bag of powder, rimmed by what remained of the original pages.

It took much of the day to go through the rest of the several South American shipments. Mr. Teddie was not about to break the method and rhythm of his work. Henry went out for pizza while they waited.

At the end, there was a modest amount of the unidentified powder. Henry weighed it on the postal scale and it came out to just over 28 pounds. Not very much for a commercial enterprise, but a lot for earning pin money working at home in your spare time.

Henry made the network television evening news and the street sales editions of both the *Star* and the *Daily News*. Both papers used pictures of Henry on their front pages with similar cutlines "Is This Man the Smithsonian Mass Murderer?" (the *Star*) and "Scruggs: Slasher or Civil Servant" *(Daily News)*. Henry thought the *Star* had the better picture (two-column head shot), but the *Daily News* was larger (four columns) and showed Henry smiling and testing the edge of his butcher knife with his thumb. NBC TV showed a still of the *Daily News* picture. Henry didn't catch CBS or ABC.

Henry hid out overnight at Phoebe's apartment, but it would not do for a second night because the Friday morning *Post* included a picture of her on the jump (page 5). She was perfectly recognizable, though many people could be counted on not to pay much attention to her face.

They caused a sensation in the Commons at lunchtime and little else was talked about throughout the Smithsonian. Without being invited, Taylor and Hamilton pulled up chairs at their table, one of those against the wall that normally accommodated only two patrons. It made it very crowded.

"Nice to have you back in town, Taylor. Have you been on vacation?" Henry asked.

"I've been away all summer. In Afghanistan. I got back this morning."

"I am reasonably certain that you are the murderer, Hamilton," said Henry while he hunted vainly for something besides fat on his spare ribs.

"But I covered my tracks, Mr. Ambassador. I certainly did. At least, I'm almost sure I did."

"I know. I can't prove it."

"Well then! It will take more than the suspicions of the Foreign Secretary to convince the press. They are accustomed to the artful deceptions and misdirections of diplomats."

"Speaking of deceptions," said Taylor, "you led us to believe you two were sleeping together. It is not enough that she denied it, but now that the press has revealed that this young lady is your mother, we can hardly believe anything you say, Henry."

"Speaking of revealing, Miss Casey, I would like to go on record that your picture in the *Post* was perfectly delightful. Unusual to find in a family newspaper, but a delight to behold." Hamilton leered just the right amount at Phoebe, and she looked pleased.

"I think," said Henry, "that the time has come to pin these murders on somebody. The press is going to want that, and perhaps even the police, though they don't usually make much fuss about murders if they're left alone."

"Would you like to confess? Or nominate someone?" asked Taylor.

"Well, I have suggested Hamilton, but he insists on proof. You really can't have it both ways, Hamilton. If I'm going to accuse you, I certainly can't be expected to provide proof as well." Henry had to be firm about this. What Hamilton wanted could set an precedent.

"Henry thinks there are two murderers." Phoebe said this loud enough so that the adjacent tables could hear her. There was an immediate hush that spread throughout the room like ripples from a stone tossed in a pond.

"It does seem like such a lot of work for one murderer."

"Henry, tell them what you told me," Phoebe insisted.

A guard came striding into the Commons, and looked around until he saw them. He approached the table while Henry was trying to think of a way to shut Phoebe up. "Mr. Scruggs? Miss Casey? Col. McKeown wants you immediately in the Under Secretary's office. Right now."

The Under Secretary was talking to McKeown, Assistant Secretary (for Museums) Douglas Cross and Dillyhay Plover when they entered. He waved them to chairs and continued. ". . . are going to have to shut down IPES until we can have a complete investigation. I don't see how we can avoid having the police in on it." He turned to the new arrivals. "Henry, Miss Casey, we have gotten the analysis report back on the powder in those packages. It was indeed heroin. We have also received the preliminary report on the body found at the zoo. It was probably female and definitely had type O-positive blood. That is Dr. Haas's blood type."

"I think we can rule out suicide," said McKeown.

"I imagine you usually can when the head doesn't accompany the victim to the scene of the death," observed Douglas Cross, familiarly known as "Double Cross" by his subordinates and more than a few of his colleagues. Henry supposed Cross was called in because he had charge of the library and IPES.

"I have been working on a suicide scenario," said Henry, "that involves getting rid of the head while chopping one's body into small pieces, but I haven't come up with anything yet. I can deal with the head by simply wrapping it and addressing it for parcel post before cutting it off. It could simply be sent to a book publisher. Such packages are never heard from again. Cutting up the rest of the body presents more of a problem."

The Under Secretary ignored Henry. "We are about to call in the police to look at IPES. Mr. Plover doesn't think we should do it because it is bound to leak out."

"I certainly do not! How would it look! The Smithsonian involved in drug smuggling! Murder is bad enough."

Phoebe spoke up: "I would agree with you if you said that the Smithsonian should not get involved with drug smuggling. But apparently we already are. How can we possibly cover it up?"

"I don't like to take Mr. Plover's part," said Henry, "but I think there may be a reason for us to go take another look at IPES before the police become involved. I have an idea that there are aspects of this affair that are more troubling than those we already know about."

After an initial, breathless silence, everybody, lit into Henry, trying to make him tell what he had in mind, but he was silent except to say: "This is something that if it turns out not to be true, you will be glad you didn't know about it when you agreed to the investigation."

"Now that is really cryptic, Henry," said Phoebe, but she knew exactly what he was talking about since they had stayed awake much of last night discussing it.

"I am not trying to be obscure, I am just trying to sort this thing out and do the least damage in the process. After all, I happen to like the Smithsonian and I'm not trying to do it any harm. It's right up there with the Boy Scouts and the NRA. Before I can proceed, however, I need a question answered. Just who was it that ordered the review of IPES?"

"I did," said the Under Secretary.

"I don't mean who asked me to look into IPES; I mean who set up the review committee, the ones who were all murdered?"

"Oh. That was the Board of Regents. The question of

saving money by cutting back on certain peripheral Smithsonian activities came up at the Spring meeting of the Board of Regents. The Regents' Executive Committee asked me to set up the review committee."

"Did anyone suggest the membership?"

"No, I just picked people who might be interested in IPES. No one advised me on it. Under Secretaries have some authority, after all."

In the end, it was the Under Secretary who decided to hold off on the police and to allow Henry, Phoebe, and McKeown to have another look at IPES. Double Cross insisted on accompanying them. After all, IPES was his own, and the latest news on the Smithsonian Murders had become a valuable and titillating social commodity. To be in at the kill would make up for having been left out of everything else.

It was after two o'clock when the investigators arrived at IPES. Mr. Teddie had not been warned. As soon as he saw Double Cross he sent Johnny to turn off the radio. "Can I help you?" he asked tentatively.

"Okay, Scruggs," said McKeown, "it's your party."

"Mr. Teddie, you know what we have found in Dr. Haas's packages?"

"You mean the dope?"

"Yes, the dope. We believe there might be something else being sent through IPES. To somebody else."

"Well, I wouldn't know about that." Mr. Teddie looked edgy. Not guilty edgy, but cautious edgy.

"I know you wouldn't. It's just that somebody apparently knew what Dr. Haas was doing and decided they had to get rid of her. What we are looking for is someone else who might be getting lots of packages and insisting that the packages be delivered to them and to nobody else."

"That could be anybody anywhere in the United States," protested Double Cross.

"No, I don't think so. Everything about the murders seems to point to them just being a purely Smithsonian affair and involving IPES. If Dr. Haas found a way to use

IPES for smuggling, perhaps somebody else on the Smithsonian staff did too."

"But there isn't anybody, that is there's not any individual," said Mr. Teddie, "who receives their shipments personally except Dr. Haas. And the Secretary, of course."

"The Secretary!" exclaimed Mr. Cross.

"What do you mean?" demanded Col. McKeown.

"The Secretary, he sends out a lot of packages and he gets a lot back. They go over to the snail lab. Several times a year he sends over a whole lot of journals and we mail them all over the world."

Henry remembered. As President of Universal Gastropoda Society, Secretary Whitfield was general editor of *Inter Nos Gastropoda,* the Society's occasional publication of learned papers.

Mr. Teddie reluctantly showed the investigators a dolly loaded with outgoing copies of *Inter Nos Gastropoda.* Henry had to prepare another memorandum, this time for Double Cross to sign, authorizing the opening of some of the Secretary's packages.

None of the outgoing packages contained anything but copies of the Society's journal. There were also a number of incoming packages that had not yet been sent over to the Secretary's laboratory. They were a different matter. The first one of a suspicious size was full of Czechoslovakian currency. There was currency in three more coming from Iron Curtain countries. There was also what appeared to be a book manuscript written in Russian.

Fourteen

It was agreed that Henry would go to see the Secretary. After all, he had the least to lose because he would eventually be going back to the State Department, assuming that it still wanted him. At the last moment, the Under Secretary decided to go along, partly because that was the best way to assure that Henry would get in to see the Secretary and partly because this whole thing was a responsibility he couldn't delegate. He was, after all, a lifelong civil servant and at an age when personal ambition seemed rather beside the point.

"You have to see Mr. Whitfield today?" asked Hannah Norton skeptically. She looked in her appointment book but that was for show because she knew to the minute the Secretary's schedule for the next two weeks. At least. "He doesn't have any free time before six-thirty and then he has to leave immediately to get changed for a black-tie dinner. I might be able to work you in on—" She looked at her book again. "Tuesday afternoon. There is a soft spot in the schedule before he goes over to the Snail Lab for his research at two."

Under Secretary Owens reached over her desk and picked up her schedule book. Hannah was speechless. Nobody had ever done that before. Owens looked at his watch and Henry checked his. Five past five. It being a Friday, and still nice weather (unless you had a problem with ragweed), most of the offices were already empty. "You have him down for dictation," Owens said. "Run her out."

"Her? There is no her. Mr. Whitfield uses a machine. And it is absolutely necessary that he have this time to work."

"Turn off his machine. If you won't, I will."

Hannah paled and scrambled out of her chair. This was something that had certainly never happened before, not even in those less orderly days before Harlan Whitfield brought her to Washington.

In a few moments she returned. "He—he will see you now," she said, trying to recover as much of her dignity as possible.

Secretary Harlan Whitfield was sitting in his southeast corner office on the second floor of the Castle. It had been inhabited by Smithsonian Secretaries since the building was finished in the 1850s. During the time of founding Secretary Joseph Henry, it had been part of the Secretary's private quarters, but within living memory, it was just what it was today, the unchanging office of the Smithsonian Secretary. Its furniture was unchanged; its occupant was in most ways unchanged. It was unthinkable that it or its occupant could be anything but the bedrock of American scholarly tradition.

"Ross, Mr. Scruggs, sit down and tell me what is so urgent that you are delaying my dinner. And upsetting Miss Norton, which is of course more to the point."

"You are having a dinner?" asked Henry.

"Not precisely. I am being had at a dinner. I'm being served up as the main course, I believe, though I can't remember where or with whom. Hannah will tell me that at six-thirty, if she hasn't quit and gone back to California by then."

"I am sorry to have upset her. I thought it quite important that Mr. Scruggs see you without delay."

"Well! Mr. Scruggs, it does seem to me that you have been stirring things up lately. Have you found another victim of the Smithsonian ripper?"

"Not exactly, Mr. Secretary. I have been looking for motives. And I think I have found another one."

"Another, meaning a motive besides the lamentable narcotics smuggling activities of our exchange librarian."

"Yes. As you know, I only became involved in this business because I was present when Mr. Smithson's bones were found in Physical Anthropology and because I suppose I am a bit obsessed with numbers and patterns. I suppose it comes from years of playing the piano."

The Secretary showed the first sign of impatience. "You don't have to explain that unless it has a bearing on the matter at hand."

"I'm sorry, I just wanted you to know that there is nothing personal in this." Henry went on with his presentation. "The murders were uncovered simply by trying to project repeating motives, in the musical sense. When we came to the apparent end of the score and looked at the whole, we saw that it had the same elements as the IPES review committee, except for one, Dr. Haas.

"That, of course, pointed us toward IPES, where the most casual of investigations uncovered a reason why Dr. Haas would have wanted to get rid of the IPES committee. We couldn't question her about it, however, because she immediately disappeared and when we looked again at the pattern of murders we found the fifth victim, Dr. Haas. This last murder was a good try, but it lacked the style of the other four. It seemed designed more to be rid of the body than to give play to a certain artistry found in the others.

"Hence, it appeared to me that the last murder was committed by a second murderer, and the first four were probably the creative efforts of a deranged Dr. Haas. It seemed to me that the second murderer was desperate but perhaps not insane.

"What could lead to desperation? Something must link the two scores. All that presented itself was IPES. So back to IPES we went and we asked wonderful, methodical Mr. Teddie which offices received packages the way that Dr. Haas had received them. Unopened and directed to an individual, personally. There was only one other."

"The Secretary," said the Secretary, "at the Snail Lab."

"Exactly," agreed Henry. He snapped open his attaché case and pulled out the package of Czech Crowns and the manuscript in Russian and placed them on the Secretary's desk.

"Oh, wonderful," said the Secretary, "I've been looking for those." He picked both up, scanned the first few pages of the manuscript and placed both in his own briefcase.

"Now I really must be getting home to change into my evening clothes. It really doesn't do to disappoint a Washington hostess. You never know when you might need her. Or her friends."

"Harlan—we really can't leave it at this."

"I know, Ross. Perhaps you can get the Regents' Executive Committee together on Monday morning. Tell Hannah what time they can meet because she will have to cancel the appointments she has scheduled for me. You won't take any other action until then?" It was phrased as a question but it was a command. "I can assure you that the delay will not cause any harm. Nobody is in danger from the Mad Murderer of the Smithsonian. Not even Mr. Scruggs."

The Under Secretary looked profoundly uncomfortable but he took such instruction reflexively after all these years. "I don't suppose there is anything that has to be reported this weekend."

"And Mr. Scruggs, I would like to give you my personal congratulations. Even though I am a biologist, I have always maintained that an arts education was not a waste of time and has usefulness in the material world. That was one of the reasons I was selected to be Secretary of this fine institution."

It seemed that weekends were chasing after one another and hardly leaving room for the workdays in between. They were made endurable because Henry and Phoebe knew they would spend them together and it no longer had to be discussed and negotiated. Still, they talked endlessly about the troubles at the Smithsonian, killing time until the next event would push the story toward resolution.

"Secretary Whitfield simply doesn't seem like a murderer," said Phoebe.

"He didn't deny it."

"Well, you were there and I wasn't." She had not been pleased about that. "But I can't believe he admitted it, either."

"Do you suppose he'll kill himself this weekend?"

"Why should he?"

"That's what gentlemen always do in English novels. They are allowed to go alone into the library and they always have a pistol in the desk drawer. You hear the bang from outside."

"Henry, you are absurd. In the first place you aren't allowed to have pistols in England anymore. And then anybody can get off from anything in this country if they have a good lawyer."

"Is that what they taught you in law school?"

"That, among other things. And that you aren't guilty until it's been proved to the satisfaction of a jury. No jury is going to want to believe the head of the Smithsonian is guilty of anything."

"I want you for my lawyer when they catch me."

"It won't do you any good. People feel different about the State Department. Henry, stop!" (Henry had goosed Phoebe to get her mind onto other things.)

Among those few who knew about the events of last Friday, almost nobody dared breathe during the morning hours while the Secretary met with the Board of Regents' Executive Committee. It was not to be confused with the somewhat inferior (hierarchically speaking) Smithsonian Executive Committee, which was made up of the Secretary and his principal assistants.

The Regents' Executive Committee was the highest Smithsonian council that could be convened on short notice, but it was prepared to deal with any sort of emergency that could not wait for the regularly scheduled but infrequent meetings of the entire body of Regents. Word quickly spread throughout the institution that something big was going on, something the results of which would be felt by everyone. It was generally assumed that it had to do with the murders. Nothing like them had ever happened before and they were bound to have this level of effect.

At lunchtime there was a long line of employees trying to get into the Commons, employees who ordinarily would not think of eating there, but who wanted to be at the heart of the rumor mill. Henry and Phoebe couldn't get in and had to change venue to the staff dining room on the fifth floor of the Museum of History and Technology. A considerable crowd of those in the know followed them across the Mall and listened to their lunchtime conversation about the proper way to cook fish. Phoebe was for fixing it with just salt, crushed Lampong peppercorns, and lime juice in a shallow glass pan, baked quickly at a high temperature. Henry held out for sliced plum tomatoes, onions, and jalapeños, or, at the very least, covering the fish with the tomatoes.

Beginning at about two-thirty, the Secretary's staff started calling bureau directors (directors of major units such as museums and independent laboratories), who in turn called office directors, announcing that the Secretary would speak to the staff in the Great Hall of the Castle at four o'clock. The Hall had already been closed to the public and a dais and speaker system were being installed. By three-thirty the hall was full and people were being turned away. The odd hush that was upon the huge two-story room with its massive supporting arches belied the number of people waiting there. The low murmur of conversation was almost funereal and grew quieter as four o'clock approached.

At exactly four, Harlan Whitfield appeared through the inner door leading from the Commons. He had come down to the main floor in the small elevator from the Woodrow

177

Wilson Center Library. He was a head taller than anyone else in the room, and his entrance drew everybody's attention. When he stepped up on the dais, it could be seen that a shorter man, Arlington Savage, Chairman of the Regents' Executive Committee, was accompanying him. Savage was a public member of the Board of Regents, but he had long experience in various agencies of the government, making it possible for him to meld the roles of the governmental and private members of the Board of Regents, just as the Smithsonian, as an institution, brought together these same sectors for research and education. Savage's presence told everyone that what Whitfield would have to say involved the Regents as well.

Spontaneous applause broke out for the Secretary. He held up his hand and began to speak.

"I have called you all here because of the culmination of events that began almost twenty years ago with the movement of a few pawns. The end game has been in progress for almost six years and I have been unable to see a way out of an inevitable checkmate. If this explanation is not very clear to you, may I say that I am not surprised. I have been trying to understand it, myself, for a long time.

"If you will bear with me, then, I will tell you a story. It began when I was a professor of invertebrate zoology at the University of California. It was a time which, in the main, I enjoyed very much. It was a great pleasure to assist in the birth of young scholars. They gave to me at least as much as I was able to give to them. Particularly, I found their enthusiasm contagious. I go on about this because I want you to understand that at forty, I was beginning to go a little stale, or at least to understand that it might, indeed probably would, happen.

"I had one student, a young lady, who was talented, beautiful, and intoxicatingly alive, vibrant. Indeed I had a dozen such, but this particular one seemed to find me attractive. I don't need to tell any middle-aged man in this room how flattering that can be.

"In any event, I committed the mortal sin of a teacher,

that is to confuse my intellectual and my personal lives. Only for a while. The young lady received her degree, specializing in my own area, the systematics of gastropods. She richly deserved her degree; she was a brilliant student. Then she moved on, married, and I rather lost track of her except through her publications that appeared less and less often, finally disappearing altogether for several years. I, on the other hand, became more involved with the international scientific community and my interests broadened considerably beyond the lowly gastropod.

"As I traveled, particularly in Eastern Europe, I became acquainted with the problems that my fellow scientists had in conducting their research abroad. As many of you know, even if these scientists obtain permission to travel abroad, it is often impossible for them to convert their money into the hard currencies necessary to conduct their research. Many times they have come to us for help so that vital research could be carried out. To the extent that we have been able to help them, we have given substance to the ideal of a single world of science without national boundaries.

"But there have been limits to what we have been able to do from the West. We have, after all, our own priorities and responsibilities. Well, one day when I was attending a conference on niche ecology in Warsaw, two East Bloc scientists approached me and asked if I would help them trade their local currency for dollars that could go into a bank account to be available for East European researchers working in the West. They proposed to use a channel which I had known and used for years and which had been accepted as a way to exchange of scholarly publications among nations for more than a century. This of course was the Smithsonian Institution's International Publications Exchange Service, IPES.

"I should say that I was not associated at the time with the Smithsonian except as a participant on the Smithsonian Council, which, as you know, is a national network of scholars interested in Smithsonian programs. But through my university, it was possible for me to arrange to receive packages forwarded by IPES. My Eastern colleagues believed that

179

authorities in their governments were sufficiently bored by the constant flow of scholarly monographs that there was a good chance that banknotes sent to me could get through despite the laws prohibiting the export of the money.

"I confess that without considering much else other than the value of such a plan to the scholarly activities of the Eastern scientist, I agreed to do as they asked.

"For a number of years, I received money from the East that I placed in accounts available to the senders. Occasionally, I would change money and send back dollars or Swiss francs when these scholars had opportunities to purchase equipment for hard currency on their own black markets. More often, I simply ordered equipment for them and had it sent to them as gifts from American institutions. Much good research has been done by very talented workers because of this arrangement.

"I would like to emphasize that I did not make any money or gain in any other way from this conversion of soft currencies. I did it solely to advance the cause of science. Perhaps I should amend that. I gained, as we all did, from the advancement of knowledge that depended upon this small assistance. But it was not gain in the conventional, 'ill gotten' sense.

"Well, after this had been going on for several years I one day received a manuscript. It was translated into English and was a novel. An accompanying letter implored me to try to get it published in the West since it was impossible in the East.

"Now, I am a biologist and literature and the publishing of novels lies a far distance from my professional competence. However, the community of a university provides friends in almost every field of intellectual endeavor. I was able to see the novel published. I will not otherwise identify it, but it was received with intense interest throughout the West, has now been published in many countries, and copies flow back into the country of origin through every pore.

"Since that time, a half dozen such books have followed, none I'm sorry to say, as important as the first, but all helping to break down the isolation imposed on the East by itself.

"Shortly before I was invited to join you as your Secretary, I was traveling again in East Europe. I was surprised to see, at a meeting of gastropod systematists, my old student who was once so much more than that. Her personal life had not been a happy one. Well, I won't go into the details, but after being some time out of it, she was trying to reenter her profession. In the course of our stay in—actually it was Bucharest—she learned about what I had been doing to help our Eastern colleagues.

"After we returned home, we kept in touch, but did not see each other again until after I was appointed Secretary of the Smithsonian. I came here and, again without giving much thought to the possible ramifications of my own little underground postal service, I moved my operations here to the Smithsonian, to the Snail Lab, where the periodic publications of the Universal Gastropoda Society and other correspondence made a perfect cover for our good works.

"Then one day, someone whom most of you know, came to me and asked for a job. She was Rebecca Haas, and yes, she was my student from long ago. I knew of her abilities, and, I confess, I was tempted by the thought of having her with me once again. So, again I did what I should not have done, I offered her a job in the Department of Invertebrate Zoology. To my astonishment, she turned it down.

"She had seen advertised in the Museum Association's *Aviso* the job of exchange librarian at the Smithsonian. She told me—she convinced me—that she wanted to work directly with the world community of scholars to expand the network of information exchanges. She said that she had been too long away from research and that it would be better for her not to try to get back into the scramble for research grant money. I knew she was right. As many of you know, before coming to the Smithsonian I served on the National Science Foundation's grants advisory council for systematic biology. I knew that nobody who was more than a dozen years away from research could ever compete for money in that sort of field.

"I don't need to tell you that Dr. Haas brought great energy and imagination to the building of science information links abroad, particularly in the biological sciences, which were of most immediate interest to me. For six years, I had no reason from a professional point of view to regret following my emotions in the appointment of Dr. Haas.

"Then during the Spring meeting of the Board of Regents, there was a general review of the cost-effectiveness of the various programs of the Smithsonian, with particular attention to those that were not tied to the core of Smithsonian interests, our research, and the museums. The Regents asked the Under Secretary to direct the review of IPES. A few years ago, that would not have happened. But now the Secretary shares certain responsibilities with the Under Secretary, and the IPES study was neither under my control, nor could I prevent it.

"For the first time, I considered the possible consequences of discovery of my little postal service. If it became generally known, particularly in Eastern Europe, that IPES and the Smithsonian Secretary were conspiring to violate currency laws and worse, to effect the publication of dissident literature, then the Smithsonian's ability to work in the East would be destroyed for decades. Not only would Smithsonian programs suffer, would be blinded in the East, but all science would be the loser. A number of excellent scholars, many of them my friends, might also suffer and even have their careers destroyed.

"I was confident, however, that the IPES committee would not look too closely at material coming into the Snail Lab and that only bad luck would bring my activities to their notice. And if I were discovered, the Smithsonian would have compelling reasons to keep the affair quiet, even though my prestige with the Regents might suffer.

"You can imagine, then, how appalled I was when the first member of the IPES committee was found murdered, soon to be followed by another and another and another. Only I had the information, I thought, that led me to suspect that Dr. Haas might be using IPES for something that would drive her to commit murder. I did not then know how close behind me Mr. Scruggs was.

"Since Rebecca—Dr. Haas—joined me at the Smithsonian, I thought I detected a certain remoteness, even secretiveness. There were times when she even frightened me a little bit. Until the events of the past several weeks, I put that down to the loss of that first bloom of affection we once had. And there is a lot of difference between forty and sixty, as there is between twenty and forty. Things could never be as they had been, for either of us.

"Well, the bodies of the IPES committee members began to be found, and I knew I had to find out whether Dr. Haas was up to something that had to do with IPES. But for weeks I delayed, afraid of what I would find out. Then, after the body of Dr. Kraft was discovered, I forced myself to act. Last Monday I searched Dr. Haas's office and right away I found what I immediately assumed to be narcotics!

"What might be the consequences of this? I could not imagine! Well, Dr. Haas returned and found me standing in her office holding what must have been several kilos of heroin. She laughed at me. She laughed and said I had a stupid expression on my face. I suppose I did.

"I told her I would have to turn her in. And she said that there was nothing I could do about it, that she could destroy my career, whereas she had little to lose. I realized then that she was not the Rebecca I had known, that she was quite mad, and, I am certain, an addict. I should have forgiven her, but I could not. The argument escalated and things were said that never should have been said. She did not seem to understand that I could not condone murder and, what I think is worse, narcotics trafficking, even for her sake!

"Well, I lost my temper. It is something I don't often do. I once did it when driving and dented a fellow's fender. I was sorry about it later.

"I suppose I ought to say that I killed her without thinking. But I remember thinking quite clearly that it was my fault that I had taken her into the Smithsonian and she had done these horrible things, and therefore it was my responsibility to stop her.

"Rebecca and I are big people, strong, powerful. We used to think of ourselves as giants and laugh about it as though we were ordained for each other. I was surprised how easily she died in my hands. Perhaps she wanted to.

"I thought about just leaving her there with the heroin for someone, and then the police, to find. But it seemed to me that if there were a chance that she would never be found and if her crime were never brought to light, it would be better for everyone. So I decided that she should go the way the others had gone and perhaps never be found at all. I cut her up in little pieces and sent her over to the Zoo for the lions to eat. Perhaps I hoped her spirit might go into the lions. I don't know.

"I understand there was too little of her left to determine the cause of death. Someone might inform the medical examiner that I found when I cut her up that I had broken her neck.

"I also hear that the news about her and the lions has upset the children who visit the Zoo. I am truly sorry about that. It was another thing I didn't anticipate.

"Now, my resignation as your Secretary is effective as of four forty-five. I didn't want to be arrested while serving as Secretary of the Smithsonian. I'm sure you can all understand that. So in about ten minutes, Col. McKeown will arrest me. We thought it was better this way to have the Smithsonian attend to its own. We wanted it to be before five-fifteen because we don't want the Colonel to have to be paid overtime. What with the murders, the Security Office is already way over budget for employee compensation.

"So, if anyone would like to ask any questions, we have a few minutes."

"Mr. Secretary," asked someone up front, Henry couldn't see who, "did Dr. Haas actually admit to you that she killed the others?"

"In a way she did. In the worst way, actually. She laughed about the murders. She said it was Wright's fault, that he

184

had discovered her trafficking and had sent letters to the other members of the IPES committee. After she killed him, she had tried to intercept the letters but she had been just a little too late. She apparently stopped Kraft in the act of spreading the news outside of the committee. Lord knows what she might have done if the news had spread further."

"Sir!" Henry held up his hand to be recognized. "I wonder if you could tell us what you did with the head?"

The audience had been growing noisy as people began to discuss the Secretary's confession with one another. But at Henry's question, everyone became immediately quiet.

"Oh, yes, the head! I forgot to mention that. I didn't want to send it out to the Zoo. A human head is rather easy to identify and it happened to be one I once liked very much. I put it in a large jar in alcohol and placed it on the back of a shelf in the invertebrate zoology storage area. It should still be there. It is with the sea anemones. I turned Rebecca's face to the back so all you can see is her hair. It looked rather like an anemone, I thought."

 **Fifteen**

People stood around in small groups waiting. Waiting for what, they weren't sure. Perhaps for the police to arrive and take away Secretary Whitfield. Perhaps that was what was necessary to convince them that what they thought they heard and saw had really happened. Many stood stiffly, unconsciously copying the pose of the somber statue of Joseph Henry that stood facing north from a plinth just across the roadway from the Castle's porte cochere. Joseph Henry, tall and dark bronze with an inevitable pigeon perched atop his head, looked disapproving, even censorious.

Henry Scruggs, Phoebe, Hamilton, and Taylor stood by themselves out on the sidewalk in front of the Castle. There were still a few tourists about, mostly college-age young people whose schools had a few more days yet before they convened for the fall term. They were completely unaware that something both dramatic and traumatic had just taken place inside the red stone Castle.

Henry wanted to go up to some of the tourists and tell them that something important had just happened. "Those tourists don't realize the sky has just fallen!" he observed to his companions.

"Don't be silly, Henry, they don't care."

"Phoebe's right, Henry, they wouldn't care if war had just

been declared," said Taylor, "and if they did care, they'd think you were the guilty party."

"Oh, my, yes!" exclaimed Hamilton. "Nobody is going to be happy until they have somebody to blame! And they can't blame the Secretary. After all he wears the cloak of Smithsonian infallibility. We'll have to find somebody else!"

"No, the Secretary won't do at all! Let's start a rumor it was Henry all along and the Secretary just admitted it because he is a good leader and takes responsibility for the actions of his troops." Taylor rubbed his hands together with satisfaction at the thought.

"They'll never believe it. Diplomats kill people with negotiation—they talk them to death. They'll never believe Henry committed an act of violence. Now if the victims' eardrums had been ruptured—"

Taylor broke in on Phoebe's observations. "They'll believe it. They'll want to believe it."

Just then the gathered and waiting staff divided and pulled back to clear a path. Secretary Whitfield accompanied by Col. McKeown, Arlington Savage, and a tearful Hannah, walked out the north door of the Castle. The three men got into the Secretary's blue Chrysler and the car pulled away and went down Jefferson Drive. Hannah turned and ran back into the Castle through the east staff entrance with clenched fists at her side.

People began drifting away. It was quitting time anyway and practical considerations such as car pools and getting a head start on the traffic jams on the river bridges got people moving.

"I think we should retire to the club," suggested Taylor. He was in no hurry to give up a good gossip.

"We could go to my place," Henry offered.

"No, I think not," said Hamilton. "We appreciate your offer, Mr. Ambassador, but our friend Taylor is right. This began at the Hotel Washington bar and it is fitting it should end there. Besides, the press won't be likely to find you there and disturb us."

* * *

187

"How could he have done it?" asked Phoebe.

"Why, he is insane, of course. Completely bonkers." Taylor gulped from his drink glass happily. "That is the first requirement for being appointed Secretary."

"I don't mean that. How could he have, uh, cut her up in little pieces without making a horrible mess. More horrible than it was already, I mean."

"The Natural History Museum is full of nice zinc-lined dissecting sinks," Henry explained. "He could have taken her almost anywhere. Probably he carried her up on the elevator to the third floor to a vertebrate zoology lab. The sinks are larger there. Rubber gloves and aprons are all over the place. But there must also be other places. The taxidermy for the big twelve-ton African elephant was done in this building, though I'm not sure exactly where."

"Well, insane or not, I don't see how he could have had the stomach for cutting up somebody he'd made love to," Phoebe wrinkled her nose to show how disgusting it was.

"Thank God," said Henry devoutly.

"Oh?" said Hamilton. "Well, be that as it may, spousal dissection is not unknown and in my research amongst primitive societies I have documented cases where people have actually eaten their lovers. It is all a matter of taste, I suppose."

Both Henry and Phoebe hurriedly finished their drinks and ordered new ones.

It took half a day to find the jar with the head. The alcohol had taken out all of Rebecca Haas's permanent wave, and her hair stuck out in all directions like the tentacles of a splendid sea creature. Dissolved blood (alcohol is a fine solvent) had stained the hair red, which added further to the unreality. The zoologist who found it, trained under the British system and learned in his Latin and particularly his Virgil, was later quoted as saying, *"Obstupui, steteruntque comae, et vox faucibus haesit."**

---

*"I was scared stiff," or literally, "I was stupefied, and my hair stood on end, and my voice stuck in my throat."

Had it not been for the Secretary's public confession, and especially the horror of the head, perhaps everyone could have done what they would have liked—they could have pretended that the crime had never been committed and Harlan Whitfield could have gone back to being the exemplary Secretary of the Smithsonian that he had seemed to be before Henry started poking around. There was, of course, the little matter of the resignation, but that could have been gotten around somehow.

Secretary Whitfield was released on his own recognizance after the preliminary hearing at the end of September. An indictment against Secretary Whitfield was handed down just after Thanksgiving. The charge was unpremeditated murder. The trial was tentatively scheduled for early summer of the next year.

During the fall season, and on into the winter, nobody in Washington was in greater demand, socially, than the former Secretary. He dined out practically every night except Sundays. So much was his popularity, in fact, that he had to buy another tuxedo and six more dress shirts to keep up with the dry cleaning and laundry. The Chancellor of the Smithsonian (who doubles, as we all know, as the Chief Justice of the Supreme Court) had to be dissuaded from becoming chairman of the Harlan Whitfield Legal Defense Fund. That honor went to a retired Associate Justice.

Phoebe and Henry were treated with an odd mixture of awe and hostility. More and more they sought each other's company, and that of the other outsiders, Hamilton and Taylor. Over the Columbus Day holiday, they set up housekeeping. It was in Henry's place because that way it wasn't necessary to move Henry's piano and besides that way Henry had to pay the rent (actually, mortgage payments), which Phoebe was old-fashioned enough to think was right and proper. Taylor had to be bodily restrained from moving in as well.

* * *

Henry and Phoebe often talked about it in bed. Somehow it seemed safer there. "How could they have released him?" Henry had asked more than once.

"He is not perceived to be a danger to the community. The judge had to release him."

"But he's crazy as a bedbug!"

"Not legally. And he hasn't been convicted of any crime yet."

"But he confessed in front of hundreds of people."

"That won't carry much weight in court. Perhaps he was only deranged when he confessed."

"Lawyers! God help us! I thought you were so horrified by it all!"

"I was. I am. But the legal system is above all that. It is sacred!"

Henry rolled over and simmered.

"I don't know why you think lawyers are so bad. Did you see the Style section of the *Post* this morning?"

"I saw it." Henry continued to face the wall.

"Whitfield gets invited everywhere. You would think he was a celebrity."

"He is. He is a murderer."

"But murderers don't usually get invited out socially."

"They do if they are important enough. Think about Stalin." Henry rolled back over to face Phoebe. This argument could go on for hours.

"In Washington?"

"You said yourself he hasn't been convicted yet."

"He's dead."

"Who? Whitfield?" Henry sat up in bed.

"No, silly, Stalin."

"Well I knew that." Henry lay back down. "He's got nothing to do with Whitfield."

"But you said—oh, never mind. I still think it is distinctly peculiar that people in Washington are falling all over themselves to invite Whitfield to dinner."

"That's Washington for you. Any publicity is better than no publicity."

*   *   *

Henry worked away on his overseas research report. By the first of December he felt he could promise Ambassador Craddock that he would have a rough draft finished by early March. He had not, however, reckoned on being assigned other work, as happened a few days later. The Under Secretary called Henry in and told him that now that everybody who could object was out of the way, one way or another, he was back on the IPES study.

And just to make sure that nobody got in the way, the Under Secretary was appointing Henry the acting director of IPES. He could begin by working up a budget and justification for the spring budget call. Did this mean Henry would no longer be working in FAO? No, it would just be an added duty. It shouldn't be too bad, the Under Secretary explained, since all the problems with IPES have been solved.

The organization was taking its pound of flesh.

It was after eleven and Henry was hurrying to get into his office while he could still claim a morning arrival—*57, 58, 59, 60, 61, 62!* Henry made it once again up all those steps to the tower and the FAO. He paused for breath. Walking to work in the cold February air had given him a little asthma and age must be creeping up on him. Or perhaps it was that he never got much rest around Phoebe. He got even less, nowadays, in the office. He looked at the secretary's desk. There was a bearded young man sitting at it. A new Temposec. A Ph.D. in history, Henry thought. Couldn't get a job anywhere else.

"Are you Mr. Scruggs?" Henry nodded. "There's a gentleman waiting for you."

"Did he say what he wanted?" Henry eyed the man's dark blue suit and the dark overcoat and hat hanging on the coatrack. They made him uneasy, somehow.

"I asked him, but all he would say was he was with the government."

With misgivings, Henry walked on into his office and hung up his own coat and hat. "Good morning," he said.

The man got up out of the chair and ignored Henry's outstretched hand as he went over and closed the door.

"Drafty, isn't it?" Henry asked to be sociable and because he didn't like to think there were other reasons why the man didn't want the door open.

"You're Scruggs?"

"That's right. This is my office, Mr.—"

"You're director of—" the man pulled a thick folder out of his attaché case and was silent for a moment while he thumbed through it. Henry looked at it curiously. There was a wide red stripe that ran diagonally across the cover of the file and large red letters announced that it was SECRET. "The International Publications Exchange Service?" The man looked accusingly at Henry.

"Yes. That is, I am acting director of IPES. Do you want to send a scholarly paper abroad? Mr.—" Henry sat down at his desk without being asked even though the other man was acting like it was his office.

"Do you send things to Communist countries?"

"Of course. Anywhere. Don't you have a name?"

The man looked in his file again. "Smith. You can call me Smith. Where do you send things? To places like Cuba? And Russia?"

"Of course. And to Albania and North Korea. All sorts of places."

"By what authority? What authority do you have to do this? Has the State Department said you could?" His manner made it clear that this kind of foolishness was just what you might expect of the State Department.

"When we started doing it there was nobody you had to ask."

"When was that?"

"Back in 1850."

"That is not an adequate reason. Are you security cleared?"

"I presume you have a right to ask?"

"Yeah, I got a right to ask."

"Of course. I'm a Foreign Service Officer. I'm cleared for top secret."

The man looked a little surprised and opened the file to make a mark inside. "Do you check the contents of everything that's sent abroad?"

"No, I'm afraid not. There must be a million pieces of mail that go out. We just send them overseas as fast as we receive them. There are two clerks working as fast as they can just to do that.

"Are they security cleared?"

"No, of course not. We don't handle classified materials."

"How do you know if you don't look?"

"We take it on faith."

"Jeezus!"

"You don't think we should?"

"We're going to shut this place down, I can tell you that!"

Taylor arrived at the head of the steps and came striding toward Henry's office. He had come to get Henry to go to lunch. He ran right into the closed glass door and staggered back holding his nose, which instantly began to bleed. He pushed the door open and came on in.

"We're having a private conversation in here, you can't come in!" the security man announced.

"Henry, who is this guy? Is he responsible for the door being shut? I'm going to sue you, mister!" Blood was running down Taylor's wrist onto his sleeve.

"Taylor, this is Mr. Smith. He's something with security, I believe. He is inquiring into IPES. Mr. Taylor Maidstone is a red-blooded American, as you can see, Mr. Smith."

"Actually, I'm a bloody Red." Taylor sat down in the other office chair without being asked. He tilted up his chin and held his handkerchief over his nose.

"Has this man got anything to do with this publications exchange business?"

"No."

"Then he has to leave."

"Actually, I am Mr. Scruggs's handler. I recruited him for

193

espionage," said Taylor through his bloody handkerchief. "So, can I stay now?"

"You can stay. Mr. Maidstone, is it? Mr. Taylor Maidstone?" Mr. Smith made some notes in a little spiral pad with a broad diagonal red stripe on it and got up and closed the door again. "Now I want you to tell me," he said as he sat down again and turned on a small recording device, "just how it was that the Communists took over the Publications Exchange Service."

"Henry, old friend, where is Taylor?" Hamilton asked as they walked across the Mall. "I thought he was joining us?"

"He was detained, Hamilton. Some fruitcake seemed determined to bring the Cold War into the Smithsonian. He came after me, but I threw him Taylor instead." Henry explained about the visitor from "the Government."

"Oh, dear! Well, I'm sure Taylor can handle him."

"I think so, Hamilton, but it does seem a bit too much, having this happen on top of the Smithsonian being beset with a serial murderer."

"Serial murderer, Henry? Oh, I don't think so. Serial murderers like to kill and kill and kill. That was not our poor Dr. Haas. *Deus Misereatur*. She certainly committed an indiscretion, possibly even an impropriety."

"An impropriety, Hamilton? I can't believe you would call four murders an impropriety!"

"Of course not, Henry, old lad! The murders were quite lamentable. But they weren't the point of the thing. Her crime was being a drug smuggler. Dreadful! Inexcusable! And an improper use of the IPES, a hallowed organ of our dear Smithsonian!"

"But, good God, Hamilton! The murders!"

"Oh, the murders, Henry. They were simply her way of tidying up after herself. Trying to keep the blots off of the Smithsonian copybook, as it were."

"Hamilton! You are putting me on! That's it, isn't it?"

"I, Henry?" Hamilton smiled. It was nothing anybody at the Smithsonian had been able to do for ages.